D1561691

DEAD
BY
CHANCE

DEAD
BY
CHANCE

PAT DENNIS

For more information contact
Penury Press LLC
Box 23058
Minneapolis MN 55423
www.penurypress.com

penurypress@hotmail.com

Dennis, Pat
Dead by Chance
Summary: Mystery

DEDICATION
The Mighty Three
Donna Seline
Theresa Weir
Marilyn Victor

ONE

Kill me," Betty whispered, tilting her body toward the driver.

"Now?" Tillie asked, pressing her foot into the gas pedal. "Or should I wait until we arrive in Deadwood?"

"How many miles?"

"Seventeen."

"I'll wait," Betty answered before adding, "unless Hannah manages to ask one more..."

"—Betty?" Hannah piped in, her raspy voice carrying throughout the tour bus like a chain-smoking hawk. "Can you tell me why the...?"

Struggling to control forty-three passengers, either coming down from a sugar high or waiting anxiously for the loo in the back of the bus, challenged Betty Chance's patience. The rest break at Wall Drug proved too much of a temptation for her clients. Not only did they purchase bags of old fashioned hard rock candies or mountains of mint chocolate fudge, they drank far too many cups of the "5¢ coffee" advertised on the drugstore's billboards along the South Dakota highway. The "free ice water" promoted by Wall Drug added to the bursting bladder issue. Once the word "free" was uttered to a group of senior citizens, a stampede of sensible shoes and clacking canes became inevitable.

Betty should know. At fifty-five years of age, she was not only a card-carrying member of AARP, she was frugal. She had to be. After divorcing her

1

cheating-gambler of a husband of twenty-seven years she found herself unemployed, penniless and in debt.

Yet, she knew she was fortunate in other ways. Soon after her divorce, she opened Take A Chance Tours, specializing in casino junkets. Her business partner was her stunningly beautiful and supportive niece, Lori. Three weeks later, the perpetually effervescent Tillie McFinn walked into her life. Tillie became her best friend, as well as the tour company's favorite bus driver, even if she was an ex-con.

Originating in Chicago two days earlier, the tour was heading to Deadwood, South Dakota. An overnight stay along the way at Harrah's in Council Bluffs, Iowa, provided a few jackpots, and the chance to enjoy the casino's Fresh Market Square buffet. Betty limited her intake to all things green and fruity. At some point in her life she'd lose the forty pounds her doctor suggested. But for now, she was aiming for as fit as she could be without adding any poundage. And that meant squeezing in her ten thousand steps a day while on tour.

Take A Chance Tours specialized in casinos and fun. Gaming establishments were dotted across the country and planning an itinerary that included a casino stay was fairly easy. Keeping her passengers satisfied and feeling safe provided the real challenge— that and the fact that Betty continually stumbled into all things criminal, including the discovery of a murder victim, or two.

"Buffalo!" an elderly gentleman yelled out, his pale, spindly blue-veined finger pointing toward the hilly landscape outside. For hundreds of miles, Take A Chance tour had driven past endless prairies, then sped along the rugged rock formations of the Badlands. Now, they were entering the legendary Black Hills, where nestled in a forested gulch, was the town of Deadwood.

2

Hannah snapped back, "A picture on a billboard doesn't count! No bingo for you!"

Betty ignored Hannah and grinned toward the seventy-six-year-old man. "Jerome, we're not playing Roadside Bingo anymore, but good catch." She brushed back a strand of salt and pepper hair from her forehead, "Hannah, you had a question earlier?"

Settling back into the plush seat, Hannah's tiny body disappeared into the cushions. In a stern voice, she said, "And it was a very important question."

"And...?" Betty waited.

Hannah shrugged. "I don't remember. But it was extremely urgent, otherwise I wouldn't have raised my hand."

Betty bit her lip to stop uttering a cryptic Really? Her too-frequent rider Hannah manufactured a question every twenty miles. The elderly sprite asked everything from "Is that a big poodle or a small buffalo?" to "What was I going to ask?"

Betty sighed. "When you do remember Hannah, just ask. But for now, let's talk Deadwood."

Overhead, the soundtrack from Dances with Wolves played softly on the PA system. The music was a salute to Betty from the driver. Betty was addicted to listening to film scores, whether she was struggling to do her daily walk or working on her miniscule-income producing blog of buffet reviews.

Holding tightly to the side pole, Betty stood at the front near the driver. The bus shifted on the winding road. She said, "A few of you may recognize the music playing. Can you guess what movie it's from?"

"Ocean's 11?" Chuck Fletcher bellowed.

Betty's eyebrow rose.

Chuck responded, "That's a gambling movie, isn't it? And we're going to a casino, right?"

Betty answered, "That's true, but Deadwood also has a rich history of ..."

"—Hangover, the movie, I mean," a second rider interrupted. "The characters stayed at Caesar's Palace in Vegas. In one of those fancy suites."

Hangover? Betty wanted to ask? No two film scores could be as different.

"Ocean's whatever, the new one with that Brad what's his name," Row 2, Seat 11 yelled out.

"Vegas Vacation!" came from the back.

"I love Vegas Vacation," more than one rider shouted out at the same time, causing a continual dialogue regarding hating or loving Chevy Chase. Three minutes later passengers were still tossing movie titles into the air.

Betty waved her hand high to garner their attention. When the chatter eased she said, "All excellent movies with exceptional soundtracks, but the music we're listening to is…" Betty paused for effect before announcing, "Dances with Wolves."

Hannah responded gruffly, "There's not a single casino in that movie. Not even a penny slot."

Betty replied, "True, there isn't, but there's a lot more to Deadwood than gambling."

"But playing poker is why I'm here," Chuck piped in. "I'm planning to either make a fortune or lose one."

"Ya wanna bet on which will happen first?" the man behind him asked.

On gambling junkets, riders bet on anything.

Eighty percent of Betty's passengers were rowdy, retired senior citizens. The rest of her clients varied from twenty-one to forty-nine years of age. And one of those riders, oddly enough, was her very own son Codey. He'd not only taken five vacation days off of work, but purchased his ticket behind her back, ensuring she wouldn't convince him not to come.

"You're being silly," Betty would have told him. "I don't need protection."

"Yes you do, Mom," Codey would have replied. "Trouble follows you around like a lost puppy."

Betty continued speaking. "Of course, many of you are already familiar with the fascinating history of Deadwood."

"Watched the entire TV series twice," Jerome said.

"I know everything about it," Chuck added, nodding his head in pride. He'd informed the entire group at least a dozen times of his B.A. degree in American History. "The Black Hills gold rush began in 1874 and the entire world made a beeline to Deadwood. I would have done the same thing."

Betty gently corrected him, "Well, not the whole world, Chuck. But, five thousand fortune seekers did flock by horseback or wagon train to the Black Hills."

"Just like we're doing, except this bus is air conditioned, and has six video monitors," Chuck noted.

Hannah grumbled, "Bet they didn't have that in their stupid wagon trains."

Betty couldn't help but laugh. Hannah always managed to find something negative to say about everything. Betty informed her, "You're right. They didn't have video monitors. But, fortunately our arrival isn't illegal like it was for the original settlers. Deadwood was still officially in Lakota hands when the gold rush began. Consequently, for decades, because the area was outside of U.S jurisdiction, the town became virtually lawless."

Chuck added gleefully, "Betty's talking opium dens, brothels, public hangings and..."

"—Murder, "Betty interjected, trying to take control of the conversation again. Before they arrived, she needed to remind her passengers of their upcoming events, as well as the procedure for disembarking the bus. She continued, "In fact, Wild Bill Hickok was killed while playing poker in Deadwood. The name of the bar where he was killed has changed over the years

5

but it's still a working saloon. Tomorrow morning, I'll lead a historical walking tour of Main Street which includes a visit to that exact location."

"Photo op!" Chuck added, holding his iPhone high in the air.

"Exactly," Betty continued. "You may also want to visit Wild Bill Hickok's or Calamity Jane's grave. If you'd like, there's always a BBQ going on at a working ranch, or..."

"—Don't forget prospecting for gold," Jerome interrupted. "Your brochure said we could do that if we wanted to."

"I can certainly arrange that with a local guide for anyone who is interested. Every day there'll be reenactments on Main Street of legendary gun battles and brawls. Plus, you'll easily be able to find free entertainment from fiddle playing to line dancing."

Hannah said in a disturbed huff, "Don't forget gambling. That's why we came on this tour in the first place."

Betty responded, "I guarantee you, slot machines and card tables will be within arms' reach. Our resort is in the middle of downtown. Thousands of slot machines and numerous cards tables, in more than a dozen gaming establishments, are situated along Main Street. In fact, our hotel has one of the largest casinos in the state."

"Speaking of the hotel..." Chuck asked, a cockeyed grin spreading across his ruddy cheeks, "don't you think the name is kind of..."

Betty squared her shoulders and fortified herself for what was to come. Chuck had already told his joke three times since leaving Chicago.

"Lame?" he said, before adding a lopsided grin, seemingly not realizing there wasn't a single laugh in response. A few groans, however, were emitted.

Betty smiled the best she could. She answered, "As many of you already know, the hotel is named after one of the most popular legendary figures in Dakota history, Lame Johnny. Not only has the 700 pounds of gold dust, nuggets and bullions he stole never been found, but according to our bus driver, his ghost is rumored to walk the halls of Lame Johnny's Hotel and Casino."

Without taking her eyes off the road, Tillie spoke into the intercom and said, "It's not a rumor. It's true. The Deadwood chapter of Ghost Hunters United proved it."

A mumbling of passengers' voices echoed in response.

Betty said, "For those of you who don't already know, Tillie's a founding member of South Side Chicago's chapter of Ghost Hunters United."

"Go Resurrection Mary!" Tillie yelled out, steering slightly to the left to let a speeding semi pass.

The busload of Chicago passengers burst into applause. The tale of the dead hitchhiking young blonde, still wearing her white party dress, was Chicago's most revered ghost story. If Betty believed in the supernatural, she may have joined in the chanting. But Betty didn't believe in many of the things that Tillie believed in—extra-terrestrials, remote viewing, astrology, and the very strong possibility that Elvis was still in the building.

Betty said, "We'll be pulling into Deadwood within a few minutes. As soon as you step off the bus you'll feel as if you've time traveled to the old west. The streets are brick and the streetlights resemble old time gaslights. The first thing we will…"

"—Oh! Oh!" Hannah interrupted, lifting her elf-like hand in a frantic waving motion. "I remembered my question."

Betty let out of a minor sigh of resignation. "What is it, Hannah?"

Hannah rolled her hand into a tiny fist and pointed her thumb toward the back of the bus. "Why is your son riding with us? Are we in danger again?"

"What do you mean again?" A worried rider seated a few rows back asked.

"Well, he's a Chicago cop, right?" Hannah's loud voice informed the entire bus. "So I figure there has to be a reason for him to…"

Betty shifted from side to side, uncomfortable that her son's private life was being discussed in front of clients. Though Codey was seated at the back of the bus, she could see deep furrows forming on his forehead.

She interrupted Hannah "Well, yes that's true, my son is a policeman. But, he…"

"Codey's a cop, like your ex-husband, right?" Hannah interrupted. Then, in a whisper loud enough to be heard on Jupiter, Hannah said, "Twenty-seven years of marriage down the drain."

Unfazed, Betty continued, "My son is on vacation like all of you."

In a questioning tone, Hannah asked, "So, you're saying your son won't get involved when you find another dead guy?"

"What do you mean by another?" asked another worrier.

Hannah answered casually, "Betty Chance always finds a corpse or two. It's kind of her hobby. Well, that and knitting."

"Hannah!" Betty said firmly. Hannah's lips clamped shut and she averted her eyes, preferring to stare out the window rather than catch Betty's laser gaze. It was obvious she finally understood Betty meant business. Hannah slid down further into her seat.

8

Betty tried to smile at the now frowning and concerned crowd. "Trust me," she said, "discovering a dead anything is not what I normally do. But when you travel as much as I do, you're bound to run into a few … incidents … and sometimes those incidents are the result of a crime. But, I can assure you that Deadwood is not only completely safe and absolutely wonderful, there is nothing to fear…"

"Except the ghosts." Tillie added cheerfully, not noticing a few of the mouths that dropped open in shock behind her.

Betty's shoulders slumped in weariness. It was going to be a long trip, after all.

TWO

The Take a Chance Tour group gathered in the lobby of Lame Johnny's. The historic wooden structure was at one time a home to stagecoach travelers, painted ladies, hopeful prospectors, and desperate outlaws. Now the only bandits hanging around the former boarding house and brothel were the one-armed kind.

"It's gorgeous isn't it?" Betty said, staring upward. A dozen chandeliers created from suspended wagon wheels, interspersed with beaming globes of stained glass, hung from the tin ceiling. Her eyes scanned the vast area as she pointed toward the rustic front desk. " area is fashioned from a one hundred and forty-five year old bar top."

Worn leather saddles hung from the dark wood walls that displayed black and white framed photographs of miners, cowboys, and Lakota warriors. At the far end of the lobby, the entrance to Johnny's Saloon was through a pair of old west styled swinging wooden doors. Throughout the lower level, the vintage dark wood floor was battered through the centuries by both spurs and high heels.

Betty's clients gathered around her, accepting keycards and asking questions. Betty gave Jerome his keycard stating, "If you need anything at all, please contact me at any time." Jerome nodded and shuffled away, his gait slow but determined. This was Jerome Anderson's first trip with Take A Chance Tours. Betty wanted to make sure it would not be his last. She extended that same courtesy to all of her clients, including Hannah. As usual, Hannah was the last to receive her room key, preferring to wait at the back of any gathered throng in order to catch any snippets of conversation or gossip.

"Here you go, Hannah," Betty said, not bothering to tell her to call if she needed anything. Hannah didn't need any reminder. She'd call if she needed anything or not.

Hannah placed the key in the side pocket of her purse and asked, "Is my luggage being delivered to my room?"

"It is," Betty assured her. "The staff guarantees all of the luggage will be in the rooms within twenty minutes."

Hannah answered, "Then I might as well try my luck at a slot machine right now, before I die in my sleep later." The elderly sprite turned swiftly to scurry toward a slot machine carousel sitting at the entrance to the hotel's casino.

"Wait! Hannah!" Betty yelled, managing to catch up with the swift moving senior. "What do you mean by saying you're going to die in your sleep? Are you not feeling well?"

For the briefest of moments, a look of confusion crossed Hannah's face. She responded firmly, "I'm feeling perfectly fine. Fit as a fiddle."

"Then why would you say you...?"

Hannah pointed toward Tillie who stood a few yards away and replied, "Because Tillie said earlier that Lame Johnny's is haunted."

Betty turned and shot a "look at what you've done" look at Tillie. The driver merely shrugged and added nonchalantly, "It is."

Hannah continued, "I tell you right now, the first time I open my eyes and catch a glimpse of a see-thru

11

prospector standing over my bed, with me wearing nothing but my birthday suit and medical alert necklace, I'll have a heart attack."

Betty couldn't help but shudder at the image of a naked Hannah.

Her perpetual client continued, "It's been two years since I've welcomed a man into my boudoir, and I've made a vow to never let another one in, not even a dead one."

This time it was Betty's mouth that fell open in shock. Two years? Not, a thousand? Betty's shock wasn't based on Hannah's age. Seniors had sex. Period. But, it was, well, Hannah's personality. Wouldn't she at least have to like someone to have that happen? Hannah didn't like anyone or anything.

She could hear Codey's baritone laugh bounce off of Tillie's giggles at the woman's comment.

Betty said, "Hannah, tell you what, I'll see if I can get Tillie to cast a spell that will keep the ghosts away from your room."

Hannah's beady eyes widened. "Are you saying Tillie is a witch? As well as being a bus driver?"

"No, I didn't say that … I was only kidding …" Betty stopped because Hannah scurried away. Hannah's interpretation of what Betty said was too juicy not to share, even if it didn't have a thread of truth attached.

Of course, Betty had been merely joking. Frustrated, she stepped toward her son and Tillie, who each had their arms wrapped around their middles to suppress their laughter. Her son's normally stern bulldog of a face had a smile as wide as the moon.

"Mom, don't tell me you have to deal with her on every trip?" Codey asked.

"Usually," Betty answered. "Hannah acts like she hates being on our tours. Honestly, I think she loves every single moment."

12

Tillie added, "And even though we have to act like we love her, we actually …" The driver paused before admitting sheepishly, "…do kind of love her. Yet, at the same time we …"

"Do not," Betty and Tillie managed to say in unison.

Betty shifted her shoulder bag strap and asked, "Tillie, what are your plans for tonight?"

Tillie loosened the navy blue tie that she wore over her crisp white shirt. Her navy blue jacket was already unbuttoned. She said, "First thing I'm doing is changing out of my work clothes."

"After that?"

"Getting into my other work clothes," Tillie answered.

Betty said, "Are you talking…?"

"Yep," Tillie said, her eyes twinkling. "My ghost busting get-up."

"And you made it yourself, right?" Betty asked, still in awe of Tillie's earlier description of it being an eye-catching combination of high style and high tech.

"I did!" Tillie answered exuberantly and then directed her next words to Codey. "It'll remind you of Bill Murray in Ghostbusters, except with way more cleavage and way less material."

Codey responded, "Uh, huh. And you say you wear this outfit in public?"

Tillie answered, "Sure. Well, usually only at the U.G.H. club meetings, but definitely when I search out entities from beyond. To tell you the truth, most of the club members prefer dark colors. So, I'm pretty sure my outfit gives me an edge."

Codey asked skeptically, "Why is that?"

"Well," Tillie said in all honesty, "I figure some ghosts might like looking at a good pair of jiggling boobs. After all, even though they're dead men, they're still men."

13

By the look on her son's face, Betty could tell he could no longer control himself. She braced herself.

He sputtered, "Good God, Tillie, you don't actually believe that crap about ghosts being real?"

Yep, Betty acknowledged to herself, in some ways Codey was like his dad. Abrupt and to the point.

The driver answered with a twinkle in her eyes. "Sure I do. The existence of ghosts has been documented throughout the ages. I read on the web a Neanderthal painted an image that looked like Casper the Friendly Ghost."

"Well, if it's on the Internet, it has to be true," Codey said.

Tillie didn't bother to take offense at Codey's patronizing tone. She wasn't about to let anyone discourage her from her beliefs. Tillie looked at Betty and said, "Don't worry Betty. I've had more than one person try to convince me that believing in ghosts is a bunch of Maloney."

"Don't you mean malarkey?" Codey asked, not used to Tillie's continual misspeaks.

"Nope, I'm pretty sure it's Maloney. My mom said that phrase was about the neighbor family. Couldn't believe a single word a Maloney said," Tillie answered.

Codey was about to speak again when Betty lifted her hand in such a way that her son knew not to bother questioning her friend's scattered logic.

Tillie continued, "Besides, not only is history on my side, but so is science." Tillie unzipped her bag and pulled out what looked like a handheld electronic meter. She beamed saying, "I bought this off of Amazon for only $19.95 plus shipping."

"And it is …?" Betty asked, knowing whatever Tillie's answer would be, it would be borderline ditzy.

"Gosh, you don't recognize it?" Tillie sounded surprised. "It's a state of the art Ghost Meter EMF

14

sensor. Like the ones the ghost hunters on cable television use."

Betty apologized. "Sorry, but I haven't seen any of those shows. What does EMF stand for?"

Tillie answered, "Electromagnetic fields. In layman's terms, it picks up the electrical vibes a ghost sends out."

Codey's practical mind took over. He asked, "Someone actually manufactures that thing for hunting ghosts? Isn't the market rather small?"

"You'd be surprised how big it actually is," Tillie answered. "An EMF is also used to diagnose problems with wiring and or get readings on power lines. Fortunately, for folks like me, it helps to establish if a ghost is in the room."

"And for only $19.95?" Codey questioned with a hint of sarcasm.

"Amazing, right?" Tillie answered, hearing only what she wanted to hear, a rosy outlook. "I have other equipment as well. Sort of your basic spook-seeking kit."

"Right," Codey responded, but this time his voice sounded almost caring, like the sort of tone one would use with a demented, sweet relative.

Betty asked, "Codey and I plan to catch a bite to eat. Want to join us?"

Tillie shook her head. "Thanks, but no. I need to take a nap. I'm getting together with the local chapter of G.H.U. at eleven-thirty."

Betty asked, "You're meeting right before the witching hour, eh? Does that mean you're going hunting tonight?"

"Maybe. Depends if we have enough spirits, both kinds." Tillie winked and headed toward the bank of elevators.

Codey stood next to his mom shaking his head. It was the longest time he'd spent chatting with the bus driver.

Betty asked, "Now do you see why I like her?"

Codey had never been a fan of Tillie. Though he hardly knew the woman, he constantly reminded Betty that her bus driver and good friend served ten years in prison for not only armed robbery but for shooting out tires on a cop car. Unlike his mother, Codey rarely believed that people could change.

"Well, yeah, I guess I can," Cody said. "I mean she certainly is unique and …"

Betty interrupted "—has a heart of gold. I'm hoping you'll get to know her better on this trip. Tillie could be the sister you've never had."

"Ha," Codey responded. "I never wanted a sister or a brother. I liked being an only child. Not only did I get you and dad to myself, I didn't have to share a single Christmas present."

"That's for sure. The mountain of gifts under the tree were yours and yours alone to enjoy. "Betty motioned toward the elevator. She asked, "Want to go to your room first? Or should we head to..."

Betty stopped speaking mid-sentence when the hotel's power went off. For a brief moment the lights flickered and then went completely dark. Even the sounds from nearby slot machines no longer assaulted her ears. Within seconds however, the power was back on and everything returned to normal. Betty dismissed the occurrence. Old hotel, old wiring.

Codey didn't seem to notice. He said, "Let's eat, first. I'm starved."

Like his mom, Codey loved food. Unlike her, he was at his perfect weight for his height of 6' 2". The myth of the overweight cop was a thing of the past. Most people in law enforcement were still at the same level of physical fitness as when they passed their

16

fitness requirements. Unlike Betty, who struggled to lose weight and always forgot to exercise, Codey had a few marathons under his belt.

"Buffet or the hotel diner?" Betty asked.

"What do ya think?" Codey asked, before adding a lopsided grin.

Betty didn't respond. She knew her son well. The two headed to Blackie's Buffet, located near the hotel's gambling floor. The sign posted outside its doorway boasted "Voted #1 Buffet Ten Times in A Row". Unfortunately, the poster didn't bother to list who did the actual voting. By the time the duo reached the buffet's entry there were only a few patrons standing in line in front of them.

Codey reached into his pocket and pulled out his wallet.

Betty said, "Codey, put your money away. I can write our dinner off as a business expense."

Codey focused his eyes into a squint. "Is that legal, Mom?"

Betty shuffled her feet. Her son! Always the cop. She said, "Well, yeah for me it is, but probably not for your meal. But still, I can afford to pay and ..."

"Mom, I'm a twenty-eight-year old man. I don't care if you can write everything off, I'm paying. Of course, if you want a different kind of son, I can quit my job, smoke weed and move into your basement to play video games all day."

Betty gave in. "Alright, and thank you."

If she and her husband ever did one thing that was right, it was rearing their son. Codey was a fine and caring man, even if he was judgmental at times.

Codey inhaled deeply. "Is that chili I smell?"

Betty answered, "You bet it is. Blackie's chili con carne is famous. And wait until you try their pineapple upside down cake."

Codey scoffed. "Pineapple is a western food?"

"Far west." Betty nodded then concurred, "Like thirty-five hundred miles west."

She was about to tell Codey about the homemade sunflower seed ice cream Blackie's featured when a middle-aged, hefty woman bumped into Betty with full-force. The lady was dragging her gigantic wheeled luggage behind her. If Codey hadn't caught her, Betty would have hit the ground hard.

The woman paused in mid-flight. "Sorry," she said, her apology hardly sounding sincere.

"No problem," Betty replied, trying to sound cheerful. Every second Betty was on tour she worked on displaying a positive attitude.

Through tightened lips the woman warned, "Well, you better be careful is all that I can say."

Codey immediately stepped in front of Betty. "Are you threatening my mom?" He asked, his voice bellowing throughout the lobby.

The woman softened. "Not at all. I was warning her to be careful. Sorry if I came off as gruff, but my purse was stolen from my room. And to top that, this frickin' place is haunted. Just be on the lookout, is all I'm saying. As for me, I'm checking into the hotel next door."

The woman stormed off, using a cuss word to cushion each step.

"Wow, Mom," Codey said. "Do you always attract trouble? Or do you simply choose the wrong hotels?"

Betty replied, "Not at all. I know it may seem like I do, but truly, stuff like that rarely…"

As soon as the first shriek occurred, Betty stopped talking.

A twentyish looking platinum blonde with streaks of pink highlights and wearing a glittery, black spandex mini dress and silver needle stilettos raced toward the front desk. Even standing across the vast interior Betty could hear what the woman screamed at

18

the desk clerk. "He's dead. Why can't you understand me? Like not breathing kind of dead?"

Codey crossed his arms firmly in front of him and stared down at his mother. "Mom?" He asked in such an accusing tone that it demanded an immediate explanation.

Betty tried to smile but failed epically. Speaking in a low voice she said, "Well, maybe a little trouble comes my way, here and there."

THREE

Codey placed his baseball glove sized hands on this mother's shoulder and led her to the nearest settee. "Stay here!" he instructed. "Do not move."

Betty released a long sigh of resignation. Sitting down, she asked, "Son, do you think you should get involved? Your jurisdiction ends at the Chicago city limits."

Codey didn't bother to answer. Instead, he streamlined it to the wailing woman. Codey was like his dad in more ways than one. He'd do what he wanted, even if it meant stepping over boundaries. By the time Codey reached the distraught female, a security guard was leading her to the bank of elevators. Codey followed in pursuit, all the while talking to the guard.

In a town the size of Deadwood, it would be only a few minutes until the paramedics and police arrived. But even a few minutes with an active slayer on the loose could turn one death into a massacre. Security needed all the help it could get, even if it was from law enforcement on vacation. Who knew what would be discovered in the room. If someone was murdered, the murderer might still be in kill mode.

Betty had no idea how the local police would react to a big city cop stepping into their world, once they arrived at the scene. It could go one of two ways. Her son could be seen as a much-needed resource, or an intruder.

She was at a loss for what to do. If Codey hadn't been with her, she would have been the one hovering around the crime scene, trying to find any scrap of information. She wasn't nosy, but urgently needed to know if her clients were in imminent danger. If there was a chance of danger to her clients, she'd round up the entire lot and head back to Chicago.

But now, all she did was sit there like a, a ... what? A helpless old woman?

No way, Betty decided. Just because her son was on the trip with her, she still had a job to do. And part of that job was protecting her riders. Within a minute, she found herself leaping into the elevator with the security guard, her son and the sobbing blonde.

Codey whispered gruffly at Betty's surprise entrance, "Mom!"

She whispered back, "I have to know what's going on. I'm here on business. You're the one who's supposed to be on vacation."

Check mark! First family squabble of the trip.

Codey nodded sideways toward her and looking embarrassed, announced, "This is my mom." A quizzical look came over the guard's face, as if suddenly doubting the man's claim to be in law enforcement.

A cop traveling with his mommy?

Less than a minute later, a ping sent out an alert the elevator had reached the third floor, the highest in the hotel. As soon as the brass doors slid open, the entourage rushed down the hallway and stopped at the very last room, the one next to the emergency stairwell.

The security guard, whose brass nameplate proclaimed him to be Joe, used his keycard to open the door. The four entered the room carefully as Joe stated loudly, "Do not touch a thing."

21

Betty was shocked the guard actually allowed Codey and her to follow him into the room. But, by then her arms were wrapped around the young woman's shoulders, guiding her every step. The female leaned into Betty for support. Joe may have felt it was easier to let another woman provide assurance.

Room #371 turned out to be what was advertised as a "suite" in the brochures. A larger than normal main room included a tan loveseat, two stuffed tapestry armchairs, and a king sized bed covered in a fluffy white duvet. The sliding doors to the walk-on balcony were opened. Sheer green curtains moved back and forth in the warm breeze coming off of Main Street. But it was the corner en-suite whirlpool bath, one large enough to accommodate two guests that held everyone's attention.

Two champagne glasses sat along the edge of the tub, along with an open bottle of Cristal in a silver ice bucket. The water reached the top of the bath where tiny soap bubbles danced across the surface. The smell of lavender bath salts mixed in with the scent of burning flesh. The half-submerged dead man, sitting in the center of the bath, gripped a clock radio that was halfway covered with water. It looked as if for the briefest of moments, he planned on tossing it as far away as possible.

"Is that your husband?" Betty asked gently.

"No. His name is Alexander Johnson, I think. That's what he told me online," the woman responded weakly.

As in Alex Johnson? Hmmm? Betty wondered. The Alex Johnson hotel was the most historic hotel in South Dakota. If the man wanted to conceal his true identity, he should have come up with a less obvious pseudonym. Maybe the man was stupid enough after all to accidently kill himself by grabbing the alarm clock while sitting in a whirlpool.

22

The young woman continued. "He's a guy I met through Craigslist. He said he'd be in Deadwood for business, and wanted … company."

That would explain the woman's choice in fashion. The ensemble was a little too sexy for casino wear in the Dakotas. She was dressed for working the streets in Las Vegas.

Looking skeptical Joe asked, "How did you get into the room if he was already dead when you got here?"

The woman answered, "He texted the door would be unlocked. Said to push it open and walk in."

Joe looked her up and down slowly before asking gruffly, "You got a name, sweetheart?"

Betty cringed at the disrespectful tone coming from the short, chubby man. He said the word sweetheart like it was a synonym for loser.

With a look of embarrassment, she said, "Wyoming Nevada. That's what I go by. It's my stage name."

Betty assumed the stage the woman mentioned included a pole. Betty took a moment to glance around the room. No matter how hard she tried, Betty couldn't suppress the amateur sleuth that claimed permanent residency inside of her. The possibilities of why a man was found in a bathtub by a paid escort were endless.

Betty began to calculate the clues. The sliding door to the balcony was open. True, it was a three-story climb from the ground up to the railing, but not that far of a climb down from the roof. Otherwise, everything else seemed perfectly normal. Basic hotel furniture and a pair of pants, a shirt, socks and underwear were lying in a heap in front of the whirlpool. What appeared to be the man's driver's license, two credit cards and a few bucks were scattered on the nightstand. If Betty could have sidestepped to take a closer look at his ID, she would have. It was one thing to call yourself Alex Johnson, but another having identification to prove it.

On the rim of the tub sat an opened jar of bath salts, which could explain the lavender scent in the air. Luggage was sitting wide open on the bed stuffed with clothes and toiletries, scattered about as if someone had rifled through the items.

Codey broke the silence. He asked gently, "Wyoming, what is your real name?"

"It was Amy Thielen," she answered quietly. "I changed it legally when I turned eighteen."

The police burst into the room, followed by a team of paramedics. Betty and Codey stepped back from Amy. The paramedics quickly declared the man dead. It only took a minute more for the police to establish that neither Codey nor Betty had any right to be there. After noting their names, occupations, and cell phone numbers on a small notepad, Sheriff Buckley instructed the two to leave. The only attitude the Sheriff portrayed toward Codey was that of disdain. It was obvious he didn't want anyone else butting into his business.

Betty and her son exited the room. In silence, they headed toward their original destination, Blackie's Buffet. Not only was Betty in the mood for comfort food, she needed it. So did her son.

Betty carefully buttered a miniscule portion of warm Jalapeño cornbread. Her plate was piled high, but this time it wasn't a bounty of low calorie vegetables and steamed fish. Betty accepted the fact that there were times in life when overeating was a perfectly sane thing to do—like when you're at a wedding or it's your birthday. Or when you find yourself, once again, however so slightly, connected to a murder.

"So what do you think?" Betty asked her son, whose plate was piled equally high with goodies.

24

"About what?" he asked. "The dead guy in the tub? Was it a murder? A suicide? Or about your driver's insistence that ghosts are not only real, but have checked into this hotel? Or do you want to know what I think about the fact that the only man in my mom's life usually turns out to be a dead one?"

Looking sheepish Betty said, "I was asking about Blackie's. What you think about the food?"

"It's okay," He answered brusquely. Then, his attitude seemed to soften. Food does that to a person. "Well, no actually, it's excellent. I can see why you were excited to eat here."

"And to write about it." Betty already knew she'd give it a five popped button rating on her blog. Early on in her blogging career, she rejected the traditional one-to-five-star rating given by reviewers. Doing a rating on a buffet's ability to pop your buttons, because the food was too good to stop eating made more sense to her.

Codey finished off his hunk of fry bread. His fingers grabbed a wooden skewer of deep fried lamb cubes. "This shish kabob is fantastic."

"It's not a shish kabob," Betty answered.

Codey gave her a quizzical look.

She explained. "In South Dakota cubed meat on a stick or a toothpick is called chislic. The bars usually serve it with a few packs of saltines and a mug of beer."

"And the difference between this and a shish kabob is …?"

Betty answered honestly. "None that I can see, or taste. But trust me, the residents of this state insist chislic is different. Every region has its own variation, using different spices or marinades." Betty chuckled, the popular cuisine reminded her of Minnesota and its hotdish—no, it's actually a casserole—obsession. "So when in Rome…"

"—Eat chislic," Codey answered, picking up a skewer of cubed grilled beef.

Betty and her son were beginning to relax, finally. Walking into what would most likely turn out to be a murder scene, and not a suicide, had been disturbing. Though there was a slight chance that "Alexander Johnson", or whoever he was, took his own life, Betty doubted it. An encounter with a beautiful woman was something most men, no matter how depressed, would not deny themselves.

Betty glanced around. A few of her clients were eating nearby. On her way to the various food stations she chatted with a few clients. But Deadwood would be different than most of her tours. Too many casinos and food opportunities were within a short walking distance. Her riders would be scattered all over town. Fun for her clients, but it made keeping an eye on them difficult.

"Are you having dessert?" she asked.

"Sure. What do you suggest besides the pineapple upside down cake?"

Betty asked, surprised, "You don't want a slice of that?"

"Oh, I'll have one. But, what else should I try?"

Betty answered, "Anything made with sunflowers. They're grown in abundance in this state. There's Sunflower Seed Butter Cookies, Sunbutter Ice Cream made from sunseed butter, and German Swiss Chocolate Sunflower Cake."

Betty stopped herself from talking. She could go on for hours about each dish available, its origins, the different variations that could be created, the minute details of its preparation. Her son loved food, but only to a point. He wasn't a foodie like she was. That was one of the reasons she wasn't taking notes and scribbling down thoughts about what she tasted. She'd come back later on the trip and sample the dishes she wanted to review for her blog. She'd also review breakfast at Blackie's. There wasn't a single bad word that could be written about buttermilk syrup.

Codey set the skewer down and pushed back his plate. With a sigh, he said, "Mom, I need you to promise me something."

Betty didn't bother to wait for her son to explain. "I will not get involved in the investigation into Johnson's death. I promise. But I want an assurance from you, that you won't either."

Codey answered, "I won't. I'm on a vacation, remember?"

"I do," she said though she knew it was more of a keep – an – eye – out – for – your – crazy -mom vacation. "Too bad you didn't bring Christine, I think she'd enjoy it." Fortunately, Betty adored Codey's longstanding girlfriend.

"She would," Codey added. "Christine's a lot like you. That's probably one of the reasons I love her."

A clank erupted from Betty's fork when she dropped it on her plate. This was the first time she'd heard her son mention the word love when talking about his sweetheart.

She worked on regaining her composure and asked, "That's good, isn't it?"

"Yeah, Mom, it is. Actually, I've asked Christine to marry me and she said…"

An eardrum-piercing screech interrupted Codey's life changing announcement.

Standing right next to their table, Hannah said, "Betty Chance! You found another one, didn't you? Another dead guy!" Hannah tapped her cane on the grey tiled floor for emphasis. "If Tillie's going to break any curse, maybe she should work on the one that's following you around."

27

FOUR

In the hotel's mirrored wall outside Johnny's Sister's Saloon, Tillie checked her reflection. Her red, curly hair was pulled together at the top of her head, held together by a glittery, ruffled scrunchy. Ghost shaped silver earring studs purchased at a Supernatural Expo glistened on her lobes. Black leather, knee high boots encased her feet. Her skintight, tan suede jumpsuit was unzipped low enough to reveal a suggestion of tantalizing sparkling boobs, thanks to glittery body lotion. Her outfit displayed without any hint of shame every mountain and valley the voluptuous yet diminutive woman possessed. A black leather belt circled her small waist while a small, black backpack hung over her shoulders. Somehow, Tillie managed to make wearing a backpack sexy, the straps miraculously pressed her breasts better than the priciest push up bra, revealing cleavage that longed for escape.

Unlike the original movie's gigantic backpack worn by the three male stars, Tillie's pack was small. There was only room for a small notebook, pen, thin plastic rain poncho, an EMS sensor ghost meter, a bottle of SpiritsBGone, a tube of lip gloss, and one travel-sized can of Aqua Net hairspray. Although Tillie was on a paranormal quest, she was still a South Side Chicago gal. Her priority was sex appeal first, and contact with beings from the afterlife second.

"Tillie? Tillie McFinn?" a male voice yelled over the din of patrons, the sound of a live western band and the electronic dinging of fake coins dropping into slot machines. The senior citizen motioned for Tillie to join him. She pushed her way through the crowded saloon. Her outfit and swaying hips incurred more than a few wolf whistles along the way. Nearing the table, Tillie recognized the man who had beckoned her. Earlier, she'd taken the time to memorize all of the Deadwood chapter members' faces, names and credentials from their website.

Slipping onto a wooden chair, she said, "You're Sargent Jack Thorpe, right? You captured the Mount Rushmore ghost on your camcorder."

He beamed with pride. "I did. Twelve seconds of undeniable proof instantly uploaded to YouTube."

Tillie added, "And you're also the chapter's president."

"Since day one," he answered. "All twelve years."

"And you go by Sarge?" She added.

Sarge nodded. "That's right. I was stationed at Ellis Air Force base for twelve years. After I left the service, the name stuck."

"But you're not originally from here?" Tillie asked.

"Nope, I eventually married a local gal and it seemed only right we stay. Besides, this land is too ripe with paranormal activity to leave. I'd feel unpatriotic, if I did."

Tillie asked, "How's that?"

Sarge answered proudly, "Capturing a ghost is no different than tracking down an enemy. I consider it my duty."

Tillie focused on the man sitting across from her. If he were there alone, she'd be flirting with him, non-stop. Hell, by now she'd be leading him to her hotel room.

29

"And you're?" She wanted to say Kevin Costner. Except for being a few inches taller and decades younger, the man was the spitting image of the movie star.

"Evan Rogers, a virgin when it comes to finding ghosts," he said as his blue eyes twinkled with hints of wicked mischief. He added, "Of course, that may be because I don't believe in them."

Sarge explained, "I've tried to convince Evan to join the club. I figure once he sees a spirit for real, he'll become a true believer. Gotta say though, it was pretty easy to get him to come to this meeting. All I had to do was to show him your picture on the website."

Tillie found herself blushing, which was unusual. But, men who looked like one of her favorite movie stars rarely walked into her life.

Evan responded, "You've got to forgive Sarge. The old coot wants me married and tied down."

Especially tied down, Tillie thought and then chastised herself for having such titillating thoughts while at a meeting of G. H. U. members.

Tillie asked, "So, what's the plan for tonight? Are we going to spend the time getting to know each other? Or will we get to go on a little hunt?"

"Actually, we plan to do a lot of ghost hunting over the next few days, if you're up for it," Sarge answered. "We need it for the article. Evan's a writer for the Dakota Daily. He plans to do an article about me taking a city slicker on a chase."

Tillie chuckled. It was the first time anyone referred to her by that name.

Evan asked, "You're from Chicago, right?"

"Born and bred," Tillie answered, proudly.

"And you won't mind being photographed," Evan asked, pointing toward a digital camera that sat next to him.

Tillie answered, "Not at all, but I think it would be more impressive for your readers if you take a photo of the ghosts we will encounter."

"Way to go, Tillie!" Sarge laughed, his veiny fingers curling around the handle of his beer mug. "I totally expect you to give Evan a hard time."

Evan leaned back in his chair, and clasped his large hands behind his head. His broad shoulders and exaggerated biceps nearly ripped through his shirt. "Tillie, the first thing you need to know is to disregard half of what Sarge says."

"Only half?" the sergeant teased. "Wow, my status has risen in your eyes!"

Unabashed, Evan continued, "The second thing I'm impressed with is your sincerity. You believe in this stuff, don't you?"

"One-hundred and a half percent," Tillie answered. "Saw my first ghost at ten years of age."

Evan's eyebrow rose in skepticism.

Tillie explained. "I'm not saying it was Resurrection Mary herself, but…"

"—Wow," Sarge responded instantly. "I'd love to see her! I even thought of taking a trip to Chicago to catch a glimpse." Sarge tossed back a gulp of beer before adding, "And speaking of females, I hope this isn't sexist. Well, seems like half the stuff an old guy says nowadays is..., but I love the outfit you're wearing."

This time it was Evan who was embarrassed. He shot a look of *That is sexist!*

Tillie didn't take offense. She said, "Thank you. I designed it myself."

Sarge added, "It kind of reminds me of Bill Murray, if he was one of those transgender people."

Evan emitted a low moan of humiliation.

31

Tillie however, took Sarge's comments as a compliment. She said, "Actually, that's the look I was going for!"

Pointing towards his plaid shirt, Sarge said, "I'm afraid South Dakota folks are a little more subtle in their ghost chasing apparel."

"Subtle is a word that's never been connected to anything about me," Tillie added. "Are any of the other members coming tonight?" Fifteen members were listed on the club's website.

Sarge said, "Nah, there's a little league baseball tournament and a middle school soccer match. You can't compete with something like that."

Tillie nodded in understanding. "Like we always say in our chapter, family before spirits, even though they're often the same."

Evan asked, "Who's this Resurrection Mary you mentioned earlier? Am I supposed to know that name?"

Tillie said, "Only if you've read books on ghosts that haunt Chicago, or have Googled her. The proof of Mary's existence is all over the web."

Evan scoffed, "Well, if it's on the Internet then it has to be true, right?"

Do all skeptics use that argument? Tillie wondered, remembering Betty's son had said the same thing earlier.

Evan added a grin that lit up the room like it was a Hollywood movie set. Tillie instantly forgave him for his doubting nature. She forced herself to focus on Sarge and to stop planning her and Evan's eventual honeymoon.

Tillie said, "Can I ask what equipment you have with you, Sarge? Your pack is way bigger than mine."

Sarge pointed toward his black, canvas backpack hanging off the side of his wooden chair. He said, "I have your basic EMF sensor, a 35 mm camera, tape recorder, and a GPS to pinpoint the precise time and location of the encounter. Also, yesterday I bought me a thermal imaging camera."

Tillie's eyes widened. "Wow, that is one pricey piece of equipment."

Sarge shrugged. "It's a tax write-off. I earn a few bucks at ghosting."

Evan's scraggly face scrunched up in disbelief. "Sarge, you never mentioned you get paid for ghosting."

Tillie answered instead. "Why wouldn't he get paid? Sarge is the best paranormal investigator in the Dakotas."

Sarge shrugged as if it was no big deal. "Actually, this past year I was hired to remove a ghost from this very hotel."

"Was it Lame Johnny?" Tillie said, her excitement making her question sound like a squeal.

Sarge shook his head back and forth. "Not him, but one of the town's original upstairs girls."

Tillie didn't have to ask what he meant. An upstairs girl was the name given to the women who were sex workers during the gold rush. Many of the town's current residents were direct descendants.

"So, are we planning to hunt in this hotel, then? Or someplace else?" Tillie asked, antsy to get the evening started.

"We were planning to search here, but…" Sarge paused, "after what happened earlier, with them finding a body and all, and then with that woman and her son walking into the crime scene…"

Tillie's stomach did a flip-flop worthy of an Olympic diver. She forced herself to stop thinking that she could possibly know the two interlopers.

Evan asked, "You haven't heard what happened, have you?"

Tillie shook her head, her throat clinching tight at the possibilities.

Evan said, "It's not official yet that the man was murdered. It could easily have been suicide by clock radio."

Tillie asked, "Who did you say discovered the body?"

"An upstairs girl who probably arrived via Craigslist," Evan explained.

Tillie let out a sigh of relief. She was sad for the woman, but relieved it wasn't Betty. Her comfort ended when Evan started speaking again. He said, "The hotel manager said that when the security guards escorted the woman to the room to verify her claim, two other people tagged along. In fact, I think you may know them."

Please let it be Hannah and Chuck, please let it be Hannah and anyone one else, please let it be… Tillie prayed fruitlessly.

It took a moment before Tillie was brave enough to ask, "Who?"

Evan answered, "Betty Chance, and her son, Codey."

FIVE

Six hours after arriving in Deadwood, Betty opened the door to her hotel room for the first time. She shuffled across the carpeted floor as slowly as some of her walker-using clients. Flopping backwards onto the bed, she kicked off her shoes. Her unopened luggage sat in the far corner.

It had been a long day and night. At 6 a.m. that morning she'd maneuvered her clients onto the bus and departed Council Bluffs, Iowa. The first rest stop was at the Corn Palace in Mitchell, South Dakota; advertised as the world's only building decorated in crop art. After that, a straight shot of two-hundred and twenty highway miles while a gazillion road signs pointed the way to their next location, Wall Drug.

Once in the tiny town of Wall, her passengers scattered quickly through the vast emporium and the various shops located along the street. The scheduled time allotment for the lunch break was an hour. But, there were too many goodies to be bought or sampled for her riders to resist. It was two hours before she rounded everyone up for departure. The rest of the afternoon on the road was spent emceeing Road Side Bingo or hosting trivia games until the tour reached Deadwood. It was a typical day on the road, a lot of pressure and a heck of a lot of fun.

However, seeing a homicide victim soon after arrival added to her normal stress. Having her son by her side didn't help to relieve the pressure. At this rate, she'd never convince Codey that being a tour host was a perfectly safe and sane business for her to own.

Still, there was one bright moment in her day. Codey and Christine were officially engaged. Mother of the Groom, she thought for the first time, and tears came to her eyes.

Damn kids, they grow up so fast.

Betty pulled herself up and slipped off her jacket, tossing it on the floor. Normally, she'd hang it up, carefully. But, dealing with clients off and on all day and night left her exhausted. The news of the murder spread quickly throughout the hotel. She spent the evening tracking down as many clients as she could, seeing if they had any concerns or needs. Betty didn't bring up the whirlpool death, unless they did. Those who heard about it chalked the death up to a suicide by a frustrated gambler, or an unfortunate accident. Except for Hannah, no one used the word murder in front of her.

At that moment, Betty wanted nothing more than to escape into sleep, but forced herself to stay awake. There were a few things she had to do before delving into the luxury of slumber. She was still on the clock. In her eyes, tour hosts worked twenty-four seven.

Betty hoisted her body upwards slowly and stumbled wearily toward her luggage. She managed to hurl the bag onto her bed. Inside, a soft case contained her laptop. Within a few minutes, she was using the hotel's Wi-Fi to connect to her video chat app. A little green light on the corner of her contact list showed one of her contacts was online. Fortunately, it was the one she needed to talk to, her niece and partner Lori.

Within a few rings Lori accepted the video call, her perfect features filling the screen. Her wavy blonde hair was pulled in a ponytail. There wasn't a trace of make-up, yet Lori's full lips looked as if they were painted. Her thick "librarian" glasses perched on the bridge of her nose. If Lori had been doing anything on the net, she was more than likely searching out the latest book reviews, or writing them.

With concern in her voice Lori asked, "Aunt Betty, why are you up so late? I thought you'd be asleep by now."

Betty answered, "I'm exhausted, but it'll be awhile before I get to snooze."

"Is something going on?" Lori asked, removing her glasses and setting them to the side. A look of concern crossed her face.

"I have good news and bad news," Betty stood up and turned the laptop sideways so Lori could follow her image on the screen.

Betty took a step toward the mini fridge. She surveyed the contents until she discovered a treasure among the mixed nuts and packaged cookies. A wrapped hand-dipped piece of chocolate from the Squealing Squirrel, one of Deadwood's top confectionary stores, sat on the top shelf. Betty began to unwrap the silky goodness as she sat back down in the chair.

Lori began to tap her fingers anxiously on her desktop. She said, "Okay, give me the good news first so I can be happy for a little while."

The sweet scent of chocolate rose in the air and drifted into Betty's nostrils. She took a moment to inhale before announcing, "Codey and Christine are officially engaged."

Lori gushed her answer. "Well, it's about time my bachelor cousin put a ring on it."

Betty responded, "I agree." She bit into the truffle in celebration.

"Have they set a wedding date yet?" Lori asked.

Betty's blood sugar spiked to its happy place. She said, "We didn't get that far in the conversation."

"Why not?"

"We were interrupted by Hannah's shouting."

Lori's frustration traveled over the net. She asked, "What silly thing was she complaining about this time?"

"A silly murder," Betty responded. Though she'd used the term silly, Betty's tone reflected the seriousness of her statement.

Lori gasped before asking, "Murder? As in a man being murdered on a Take A Chance Tour? Again?"

Her niece was referring to the three-hundred and fifty plus pound dead man discovered on a previous tour by Betty and Tillie. Or perhaps she was alluding to the stiff Betty stumbled upon in Mississippi. But to Betty, both of those murders were old news, and the cases were solved and filed away in her past. As far as Betty was concerned, this latest tragedy had nothing to do with Take A Chance.

She explained, "The victim was a hotel guest, not one of our clients."

Lori responded, "Thank God. Did they catch the killer?"

"I don't think so. And I don't know if it's been officially declared a murder but…"

"Wait a second," Lori interrupted. Betty could see Lori's long fingers working frantically at her keyboard. Finally, Lori said, "Yep, it's already been declared a homicide."

"You found a news report about it?" Betty asked.

Lori responded, "I typed Lame Johnny's Hotel, the word murder and today's date. Two online sites have it as their top story. One is a news website out of Montana. The other site is called the Dakota Daily and the story on it was written by an Evan Rogers. Both sites were updated a few minutes ago."

"Is there any mention of someone being arrested?"

Scanning her computer screen, Lori responded, "No, but the Daily speculates the killer is still on the loose."

"Did they actually use the word killer? As in singular?" Betty asked, frustrated once again by the immediacy and inaccuracy of online reporting.

Lori answered, "They did."

Betty asked, "How do they know it wasn't two killers, or three…" Or a whole busload. She shook her head in disgust at her own dark humor.

Lori continued to feed her information. "Supposedly, the victim's name is Alexander Johnson. Doesn't that sound suspicious to you?"

"Of course," Betty said. Lori was as familiar with the Alex Johnson Hotel as Betty. Take A Chance booked tours that included a stay in the historic establishment.

"Anything else?" Betty inquired.

"It appears he was electrocuted in a whirlpool."

"Any personal information?"

"Only that he was married and owned a locksmith store in Sioux Falls."

"Sad," Betty answered. "I'll check out those sites later, after I work on my blog."

"Aunt Betty, before you click off, I need to ask, are you in any way connected to…"

"Not really," Betty interrupted. The last thing she wanted was for Lori to hop on a plane and fly out to her rescue. Her niece had a tendency to be incredibly impulsive.

Lori's voice turned stern. "What do you mean, not really? Shouldn't your answer be a simple 'no'?"

Betty decided it was time to share what happened. It was bound to come out anyway via the Hannah Express. She said, "Codey and I just happened to follow along with the security detail heading to the room and...we were with them when they discovered the body."

"Just happened to be with them?" Lori mocked.

Betty replied, "It's a long story. But, I promise you, Codey's and my involvement is over and done with."

"Do you want me to come out there?" Lori asked.

"No, not at all, stay in Chicago and help Gloria with paperwork. Besides, Codey's here. He'll protect me," Betty said, not adding whether I want him to or not.

"He'd better," Lori answered.

Three quick raps sounded on Betty's hotel room door interrupting their conversation.

Betty said, "Lori, I have to go. Trust me, everything is fine."

"Okay," Lori said, her tone sounding doubtful. "Love you."

"Love you too," Betty said, clicking off of chat before hustling to the door. She didn't bother to look out the peephole before opening the door.

Standing in the hallway, dressed in her ghostbusting outfit, Tillie's elbows pointed outward as her hands rested firmly on her hips. Her face was stern. Using an accusatory tone, she demanded, "Do not tell me you and Codey were actually there when the body was discovered."

"I won't tell you," Betty answered, turning around and heading back into her room.

Tillie followed in hot pursuit. She sat down on Betty's bed and said, "People are saying you and..."

"We weren't there initially," Betty interrupted. "Codey and I went with security to verify there was a body. The victim's date is the one who discovered it." Betty sat back down on the chair as Tillie plopped on the bed.

Using her fingers to produce air quotes Tillie asked, "By 'date' you mean hooker?"

"Looks like it," Betty answered.

"Were the two of you invited to tag along on this discovery?"

"Not exactly," Betty admitted.

Tillie instructed, "Tell me everything."

"I will, but I have to ask who told you? Hannah?"

"No, actually, it was a reporter," Tillie explained. "Evan's tagging along with the local chapter of G.H.U. to write a story. He works for the…"

Betty interrupted, "Dakota Daily. Lori found a newspaper story connected to it online. The Daily verified it was a murder and that the killer is still on the loose."

Tillie said, "Then Evan updated it after I left him a few minutes ago. He told me it hadn't been verified."

"He may not have known then. Besides, anyone can update a website almost immediately with a smartphone these days," Betty added while wondering where Evan got his information so quickly. Was it from Sheriff Buckley? Or a hotel employee?

Tillie pointed her manicured finger toward the table. She asked, "Is that a candy wrapper from that place you told me about?"

"The Squealing Squirrel? Yep. There's another one in the mini bar if you want it."

Tillie answered, "Nah, not now. I'm watching my figure."

In the past, Betty watched Tillie eat mountains of buffet goodies without either gaining an ounce or expressing any concern she might. Tillie weighed exactly the same as she did when she was a teenager, 125 pounds. Then it hit Betty. She scrunched up her face and asked, "What does this reporter look like?"

Tillie fell dramatically backwards on the bed, spreading her arms out like a snow angel. She answered, "Spitting image of Kevin Costner."

Betty's eyes widened. She was used to Tillie exaggerating about the sex appeal of men she encountered. "Exactly like him?"

"Exactly, except Evan is taller, his eyes are bluer, his body is better, and he's decades younger."

"Oh my," was all that Betty could respond. Tillie adored Costner, but then she adored a lot of men, good looking or not.

Tillie sat up, adjusted her clothing and said, "Too bad he's such a hunk because I'm planning on behaving. There'll be zero flirting on this trip. I'm here to contact the supernatural, not to add another man to my list."

Jesting, Betty asked, "How many boyfriends do you currently have?"

Tillie answered in all seriousness, "Honestly, I don't know. Going out for dinner doesn't necessarily make a man your boyfriend, does it?"

"No, but going out for breakfast together after the night before probably does," Betty reminded her.

Tillie stood up and announced, "If you don't need me, then I'm heading back to meet up with the gang."

Betty answered, "I'm good. Have fun."

Tillie shivered and added, "If I were you, I'd call the front desk and ask them to fix the draft in here."

Betty answered, "What draft? I was thinking about turning up the air conditioning."

"You didn't feel that blast of cold air?"

"Not in the slightest," Betty answered honestly.

Tillie rushed to a corner and stood still, her arms positioned at her side. She said "This cold spot is like twenty degrees lower than the rest of the room."

"That can't be," Betty argued.

42

Tillie gushed, "Sure it is, Betty Chance! You're so lucky! Your roomie's a ghost!"

∞

It took fifteen minutes of Betty's wheedling to get Tillie to leave the room with a vow not to return with her paranormal investigator friends. Betty didn't believe in spirits. Nor did she believe in extra-terrestrial beings, remote viewing, astrology, or any of the possibilities that her friend accepted as reality.

And if the corner of the hotel room felt like it was 20 degrees colder—and it did—there had to be a perfectly rational explanation. Besides, Betty had work that needed to be done in the present, there was no time to deal with spirits from the past.

Once online, Betty clicked on her webpage to see if any of her clients, both on the tour and off, had posted any comments. Fortunately, no one wrote about Johnson's watery demise. Most of the comments were merely wishing her well or hoping someone won one jackpot after another. One poster reminded her to be on the lookout for Lame Johnny's missing gold. Even her office manager Gloria Morgan posted, asking her to bring back a few dozen truffles.

Betty wrote "Thank you all for the good wishes. So far, our trip has been extraordinary! From a few of my clients winning jackpots in Council Bluffs to a succulent dinner at Blackie's Buffet in Deadwood. The pineapple upside down cake is one of my favorite desserts. And it may sound like an exaggeration, but it wouldn't surprise me if our riders didn't leave Wall Drugs with a half a ton of salt water taffy and hard rock candy.

43

Tomorrow's plans include a one-hour historical walking tour. And speaking of history, some of you may not be familiar with the legend of Lame Johnny, a notorious horse thief and stage coach robber. True, there were many outlaws in the Black Hills during the gold rush era but none of them stole 700 lbs. of gold that was never recovered. Poor Lame Johnny was eventually strung up by a group of vigilantes. One-hundred and forty years later, folks are still searching for the gold. Who knows, maybe one of my clients will hit more than a jackpot on this trip. It could happen!"

Betty hit Send, ruminating at the same moment that It could happen, but probably wouldn't. But hope springs eternal in the veins of a true gambler, and most of her clients fit that description perfectly.

It took Betty only a few minutes to strip out of her clothing and get ready for bed. She set the timer on her iPod for two things. Twenty minutes of a randomly selected, soothing sound track to fall asleep to, and a jolting wake-up alarm for six a.m. The iPod was placed gently in a dock on the nightstand, and Betty slipped into bed.

Closing her eyes, she waited to hear the calming sounds of ... What the heck?

Betty bolted upright. It wasn't the sound of the Titanic movie score, but a musical number that she hadn't downloaded to her iPod. True, there were over two hundred soundtracks on her iPod, but she knew the titles of every single one. The music that filled the room now was not one she'd purchased—ever. Not that it wasn't catchy, that wasn't the point. There wasn't a single rational reason why the theme music from Ghostbusters filled her ears. Not one.

Betty reached over and shut off the device. Pulling the sheet up to her chin, she clutched at it tightly and shut her eyes. No matter what happened, she vowed to not open them until morning. Even when a blast of

44

cold air traveled across her face, Betty didn't peek at the room around her. Nor did she freak out when the smell of lavender invaded her nostrils.

She'd deal with whatever was happening in the morning. If she could track down killers, solve crimes that the police couldn't, she should easily be able to figure out why her hotel room had turned into a haunted house.

SIX

You're saying he wasn't electrocuted?" Betty asked, using her fork to swirl the shirred eggs around on the plate. At eight a.m. Blackie's Buffet was filled with the din of tourists, gamblers, and the sounds of utensils being dropped into food bins. Betty, Tillie and Codey were lucky to get a table.

Tillie nodded, right before she bit into a mini sticky bun.

"And his name is actually Alexander Johnson?" Betty asked in disbelief, lifting the fork to her mouth. The recipe for Shirred Eggs was definitely going to be posted on her food blog.

"Evan verified it this morning," Tillie answered.

Betty's left eyebrow shot upwards. "This morning? Does that mean the two of you spent the night...?" Betty didn't bother to fill in the rest of her question. Her perpetually chatty friend would fill her in on all the details, sordid or not.

Tillie answered, "It doesn't a mean a thing, at least not what you're thinking. Remember? I'm here on official Ghost Hunters United business. No hanky, much less spanky."

Betty didn't bother to respond to Tillie's misuse of words, though if she allowed herself to think about it, perhaps it wasn't a misspeak after all.

Tillie continued, "Evan called this morning to let me know the group is meeting at 9:30 a.m., sharp."

"More boogeyman stuff?" Codey asked, his tone bordering on ridicule.

Tillie didn't bother to react to his tone, but nodded enthusiastically. She said, "Wait till you hear this! The victim's full name is Alexander Rushmore Johnson."

"Really?" Betty asked, wondering at the same time why parents did that to a child? It was a set-up for bullying. "Did your reporter friend mention anything else about the murder?"

Codey grunted before shooting a warning look toward his mother. "Mom, remember? We don't care how the man died, or who he was."

Betty said, "But don't you think it's kind of ironic that his name is..."

Codey interrupted. "Mom, It's none of our business. We promised Sheriff Buckley we'd stay out of it."

"Of course it's interesting, the fact that..." Tillie piped in right before Betty kicked her under the table. After mouthing the word 'Ow' Tillie admitted in a weak whine, "—Johnson's death was staged to look like a suicide, when he actually died from a blow to the back of the head? Something like that doesn't happen every day."

In a bitter voice Codey added, "Unfortunately, it does."

Tillie's eyes brightened. She asked, "Betty, did you find the surprise I left for you?"

Betty shook her head.

Tillie continued, "I figured you'd be listening to music sooner or later, so when you left your iPod on the table at Wall Drug, I grabbed it. I downloaded a movie score for you."

"Ghostbusters!" Betty replied, her voice stern before mumbling, "Thanks." She didn't bother to add

47

Tillie's prank had her believing for a millisecond that her hotel room was haunted.

Tillie grabbed a small decanter of chokecherry syrup and emptied the contents over her heavily buttered, crunchy French toast. Betty gave her a questioning look. Tillie said, "I guess you remember I said I was going to watch my figure. We'll, I've come to my senses. I will not eliminate pleasure because of a man, even if he is a stud. Eating is just too good to pass up."

"I agree," Betty responded, her elastic waistband feeling a little tighter. But, she probably wasn't the only one feeling a tug of material. The entire establishment was filled with folks piling their plate high, no matter what their size. Besides, Tillie had nothing to worry about when it came to metabolism. After the continual avalanche of food Betty had seen her eat throughout the years, the woman had yet to gain an ounce.

Breakfast was a big deal at the hotel, and not only because it was excellent. It was cheap; $4.99 for all-you-can-eat goodies. Situated around the room were five different food stations featuring various ethnic or historical cuisines. The chef specialized in using locally grown products whenever possible, often using the same utensils the pioneers had. His dedication to accuracy was one of the reasons the omelet chefs used seasoned cast iron skillets instead of a commercial, stick free pan.

Codey, pushing his plate away from him, said, "I'm getting more food." He pushed himself up, but before stepping away instructed, "Mom, talk about other stuff besides crime while I'm gone? Okay? Your speculating only leads to trouble."

Betty watched her son lumber toward the food station devoted to breads. Indian fry bread rested next to steaming corn bread, yeast rolls, drop baking powder biscuits, and hard tack. Immense bowls of various flavored butters suggested every possible speck of a slice of bread's surface was to be smothered in butter. And at Blackie's, it usually was.

As soon as her son was out of earshot, Tillie leaned over and said, "It's cute, isn't it? How your son thinks he can control you? It's like he doesn't know you at all."

Betty laughed, brushing back her salt and pepper colored bangs. "In a lot of ways, he doesn't."

Tillie continued, "But you're still going to speculate, right? There's no way you can stop yourself, is there? That would be like me trying to give up wearing leopard-prints and spandex leggings. Ain't gonna happen."

A mischievous look came over Betty's face. In a low voice she said, "Well, there are a few things that sort of bother me about the situation."

Tillie hunched over the table to catch every word. "Such as…?"

Before Betty could answer, a shrill voice cut across the tabletop like a Ginsu knife and interrupted their conversation mid-huddle.

"So, there you are," Hannah said in a tone that suggested she'd been searching for Betty since cavemen roamed the earth.

Betty forced herself to smile at her client. "Yes," she answered bravely in a practiced upbeat tone. "Here I am. What can I do for you, Hannah?"

"Nothing," Hannah responded, holding her cane as if it were as lethal as King Arthur's sword. "I like to know where you are in case someone else gets killed."

Betty tightened her lips. She said, "Hannah, I don't think anyone else will…"

Hannah interrupted again, "Or one of those ghosts Tillie talks about shows up. A woman traveling alone can't be too careful."

49

It was pointless to remind Hannah that she wasn't traveling alone, that not only did she arrive in Deadwood with forty-three other riders, Betty and Tillie were always close by, if not in person, then a short phone call away.

Trying to ease her client's fear Betty began, "Hannah, there are no ghosts…"

Tillie interrupted. "Sure there are. Betty, remember the one in your bedroom last night?"

Betty's eyes shot a speeding bullet across the table toward Tillie.

Hannah responded immediately, "I don't want to hear what goes on in Betty's boudoir, any more than she wants to hear what goes on in mine!"

For a change, Tillie and Betty turned utterly speechless at the same time.

Hannah added, "Besides Betty Chance, I've been on too many of your tours to not realize you'll eventually solve this murder. Same old, same old if you ask me."

Betty gritted her teeth. Hannah couldn't remember her room number, but she was able to remember every grizzly detail of any misfortune on a Take A Chance tour. Betty decided to answer with a white lie in order to calm Hannah down. She said, "We're not even sure it's a murder yet, so…"

"Sure it is," Hannah said. "It's all over the Internet. Someone even posted about it on your blog within the last few minutes."

Betty counted to ten before responding. The grey haired gremlin standing in front of her couldn't open her luggage lock, but was a whiz at all things social media related. In a terse voice Betty asked, "And does that someone, happen to be you?"

Flustered, Hannah rushed her response. "I better eat some food before it's all gone." She hustled toward a mountain of sweet rolls and Danish pastries.

50

Tillie said, "She's right you know. You usually do fall into solving the nearest crime."

"Only twice did that happen while on a Take A Chance tour," Betty reminded her driver. "And that was then, not now. Codey's right, this homicide has nothing to do with me, you or Take A Chance Tours."

"As far as you know," Tillie added ominously.

"As far as I know," Betty responded, crossing her fingers together underneath the table for luck.

∞

At 9:45 a.m., a small crowd gathered around Betty, listening attentively as she described the murder in grizzly detail. Standing on the sidewalk, she pointed toward the rustic, historic wooden sign hanging overhead. The words "Historic Site Saloon Number 10 where Wild Bill was shot" were carved into the dark wood.

Betty continued, "On August 2nd, 1886, a bullet ripped through the back of Wild Bill's head as he sat at a table. It escaped through his right cheek and ended up in another man's left wrist. Hickok died instantly. His assailant was..."

"Wasn't he playing poker at the time?" an avid listener interrupted.

Chuck intervened. "Sure was. Hickok was holding a pair of Aces and a pair of eights when he died. That hand is known to this day as Dead's Man's Hand. In fact..."

Someone had the courage to interrupt the alleged historian. Jerome asked "Did Calamity Jane kill Wild Bill? Was he cheating on her?"

Irritated, Chuck snarled, "Calamity Jane wasn't anywhere near the saloon. Crooked Nose Jack McCall

51

took out Hickok. Everyone knows that. McCall was tried twice and hung once."

Through tight lips Betty responded, "If I hadn't read up on Dakota history before coming here, I would have asked the same question, Jerome."

Betty faced the difficult challenge of placating one client while making sure another didn't feel slighted. Chuck was nice enough, but he acted as if he invented history, not merely studied it. Betty lifted her hand in the air to motion her clients to follow her down the sidewalk. Only a portion of her riders showed up for her historical walking tour of Main Street.

Codey was one of them. She'd tried to convince him to take the day off and explore the town on his own. Play some cards or go for a run. Maybe even check out the jewelry shops that featured Black Hills Gold. He'd yet to find the perfect engagement ring for his sweetie. He'd politely ignored his mom's suggestion and continued his self-appointed position as her unwanted security guard.

The group shuffled past various bars or casinos toward their next location, the Bullock Hotel. They strolled past a few western-style shops with intermingled offerings of pottery, hand crafted jewelry and western style clothing. If someone won a fortune with Lady Luck, they could easily turn around and spend it on Main Street.

Betty stopped abruptly when the women next to her began pointing across the brick street. In the middle of the sidewalk, wearing her ghostbusting apparel, Tillie stood chatting away to the men on both sides of her. The men were outfitted in worn jeans, plaid shirts, and stuffed backpacks. The older man held a dousing rod in his hand. Betty recognized the younger man—Evan. If it wasn't him, then Kevin Costner had drifted into town for a morning stroll.

A passenger asked, "What the heck is Tillie wearing? Is that a prospector's outfit?"

Betty answered. "In a way. But, she's not looking for gold. Tillie's out hunting ghosts."

"In the daylight?" Another woman squealed, quickly taking a look around, as if an apparition would be standing near her.

"Yep," Betty answered, not wanting to continue discussing Tillie's hobby if possible. Once the conversation started about the possibility of an afterlife, it might not stop. Seniors seemed to be fascinated by the concept, as if it were the next stop on their tour.

Betty was about to move ahead swiftly when a sinking feeling lodged in her stomach. She watched a squad car carrying Sheriff Buckley pulled up next to her friend and stopped. Buckley stepped out of the passenger side of the car before it drove away. He began an intense conversation with Tillie and her male cohorts. Though Betty couldn't understand what was being said, the body language being tossed about was easy enough for her to read.

Tillie vehemently shook her head back and forth, her curly red hair bouncing across her shoulders. Evan pushed back his shirtsleeve to look at his watch, as if the Sheriff was taking up his valuable time. Buckley kept pointing behind him, toward the end of the street. Even from a distance, Betty could tell that the group reluctantly followed Buckley as he turned around and walked in the opposite direction. Tillie's normal perky steps turned into slow motion resignation.

"What's that about?" Jerome asked, adjusting his thick glasses higher on the bridge of his nose.

Betty shrugged as if it were no big deal to watch her driver being led away by the local law enforcement. In a way, it wasn't. It had happened before.

Trying to sound carefree, Betty responded, "I'm sure it's nothing. Maybe the Sheriff's into ghosts."

Hannah opened her mouth to speak, but snapped her thin lips shut when she saw the look Betty was sending her way.

Instead it was Chuck who added, "Or Tillie's busted and her gang is going with her for support." The community college educated historian was overbearingly proud for coming up with a solution that rivaled Sherlock Holmes in its brilliance.

Betty felt her temper flare but managed to keep it under control. Would Chuck implicate Tillie in the whirlpool homicide? If he did, the group would not only remember what he said, but a few of them would share the gossip with the rest of the riders. By noon, Tillie's name and felony background would be the talk of Deadwood.

Betty felt she had no choice but to ask him what he meant. Placing her hands firmly on her hips, she asked, "For what reason?"

"What else?" Chuck asked, "Public sexiness. Did you see Tillie in that outfit? The sheriff probably thought she was an upstairs girl."

SEVEN

Twenty minutes earlier, Codey stepped away from his mom's tour with the excuse of wanting to place a wager. He'd discovered while on a gambling junket, no matter what was happening, if someone said they wanted to place a bet, not a single question was asked. An earthquake could hit, all the buildings could violently shake, but if the words, "You know, I've got a feeling about that slot machine" were uttered, the general consensus would be, "Go for it!"

Not even Hannah voiced concern as he scrambled across the street. But pulling the lever on a one-armed bandit wasn't on Codey's mind. His intention was to follow, as inconspicuously as possible, Tillie and her entourage.

His mom may have been correct in her assumption that it was nothing to be concerned about. Perhaps the Sheriff was merely curious about the spirit world. Policemen were as nutty as the rest of the population. He'd known Chicago cops who frequented psychics to get help in solving crimes or "talk" to a murder victim, supposedly.

Codey only believed in what he could see with his own eyes and figure out with his own brain. He was a lot like Betty in that way. Life to him was a math equation. You did this—you got that. Period. Actions created reactions, and not all of them good. Unlike math however, the results were not guaranteed.

Sometimes it wasn't possible to know what reaction an action might cause … like his following the group and then casually leaning against a tree, waiting for Tillie and her crew to exit the building they'd just entered.

He was wise enough not to enter the facilities. One stick of chewing gum later, Tillie finally emerged. She and her two male companions looked happy enough. She continually giggled and swayed her hips as the group headed back toward downtown.

Codey released a sigh of relief. If there was a problem, it had been settled quickly. He took one step away from his post when Sheriff Buckley emerged from the building. The sheriff placed one hand on his holster and the other he held in the air motioning for Codey to come his way.

"Damn!" Codey swore under his breath. So much for his being stealthy. Maybe South Dakota cops were as smart as Chicago cops were—or maybe smarter.

∞

Tillie clicked on her flashlight, tightened her backpack straps, and prepared to step into the unknown. On the wall next to her a light switch was turned off. A single, working light bulb hung from the center of the ceiling below her, but the assemblage of trackers preferred to explore in the dark. A sudden burst of light might scare away a spirit. A dimmed flashlight was far less intrusive.

She placed her hand on the railing and started down the rickety steps. Sarge and Evan followed behind her. As soon as her feet were on the cellar floor, she aimed her flashlight slowly around the room. A labyrinth of insulated pipes stretched out from the

56

antique gravity furnace that once was fed coal before its conversion to gas.

Tillie bumped into something hard and gulped. It was only a wooden support beam. She used her flashlight to light up the outline of the old furnace. She'd watched enough reruns of This Old House to know how noisy the monstrosity was when working. If folks were reporting an eerie sound coming from the basement, it could easily be the source.

She asked, "How did we get permission to scramble around down here? The owner doesn't mind strangers traipsing about?"

Sarge explained, "I approached him a week ago. Told him I heard rumors his establishment was haunted and wanted to bring a Chicago expert in to check."

Tillie responded, "I'm hardly an expert. He didn't know his building is haunted?"

Sarge shook his head. "He'd heard the rumors, but laughed them off. Said people will believe anything, and there's a sucker born every minute."

Evan responded, "There is."

Sarge said, "That's why we're here. I'd love to convince him he's wrong, and I'm right."

Evan moved around the room slowly and asked, "How did you get him to agree?"

Sarge didn't take offense at Evan's brashness. "Told the son of a gun it was good for business, that tourists would flock to Harney's Jewelry & More if it was known to be haunted. Told him I'd mention that fact on our website."

Evan scoffed, "Yeah, nothing says 'marry me' like a spooky engagement ring."

Tillie added, "Sounds good to me. I love anything made of gold, especially if it's spooky."

Sarge responded, "Black Hills Gold, you mean. That's the only kind Harney sells."

"Yeah, I know. Slip of the tongue."

She'd been an admirer of the official South Dakota state jewelry for years. Even before Tillie made her first purchase from a home shopping network, she was familiar with its history and beauty. One of her close friends in prison was a woman who'd received a two-year sentence for a shoplifting spree. The crime spree covered fifteen hundred miles and thirteen jewelry stores before it ended in Sioux Falls. The convict's misadventure stopped when she ran "out of boyfriends and gas".

Tillie canvassed the room, slowly. A few empty wooden crates were strewn about. She said, "Speaking of Black Hills jewelry, I love the colors. I had no idea you could turn gold rose, or green."

Evan informed her, "The man who came up with the concept of mixing gold with alloys said it came to him in a dream while he was starving and thirsty." The way Evan related the story, it sounded as if he didn't believe a word of it. Like any reporter, he was always looking for the lies.

Tillie answered, "That sounds like something I'd think up. If I go five hours without food, I start having nightmares about cotton candy and scary clowns. No telling what I'd dream if I were actually starving."

Tillie heard steps overhead. Only the owner was present when they arrived. Now it was filling up with tourists and shoppers. Their muffled talk from upstairs bounced off the cellar's limestone walls. The floor was a mixture of packed dirt and clay. The room was small, but a corridor led to other parts of the underground space. The lower level reached as far back as the alley behind the three-story building.

Tillie moved her light slowly around the rest of the room, hoping to catch a glimpse of a moving shadow or a fleeting Spector. All she saw was Evan taking one snapshot after another with the camera that hung from

58

a strap around his neck. He pulled a small voice recorder from his pocket.

Evan clicked on the device. "Since you two won't let me turn on the lights, the only notes I'll be able to take are with my recorder. Thankfully, I remembered to put in new batteries."

"Won't matter," Tillie responded as she zipped up her top to protect herself against a sudden chilling of the air. The atmosphere felt a good ten degrees cooler.

"Why?"

Tillie explained, "Ghosts like to play around with frequencies, electrical equipment, batteries, whatever. If you tick them off, they will drain your battery to get back at you. And odds are, with your attitude..."

"—Right," Evan responded sarcastically.

"She is right," Sarge insisted.

Suddenly, Tillie instructed, "Shh...be quiet. Did you hear that?"

"Hear what?" Evan asked.

Tillie continued. "A bell, like a single jingle bell ringing."

Evan answered, "Nope, didn't hear a thing."

"Me neither," Sarge answered.

Tillie inhaled deeply. She said, "And I bet you don't smell that, either."

"Smell what?" Evan responded. "The dirt floor?"

"No, the flowers." Tillie paused to inhale deeply. "They're both really good signs. She's welcoming us."

"She who?" Evan asked.

Tillie answered, "The upstairs girl, except this time she's in the basement."

∞

59

Codey shifted about uncomfortably in the creaking wooden chair, his muscular frame covering every square inch. He asked, "So, there's no specific reason you brought Tillie and her two buddies in for questioning?"

The sheriff leaned back, and placed his hands around the back of his head. He answered, "It wasn't an official questioning. I wanted to see what's going down. Evan's fairly new in town and he's a reporter. To be honest, I've never met anyone in the news business I trust."

"But, I assume you know Sarge?" Codey asked.

"Everyone knows him. He's basically a good guy, though he's a little nutty when it comes to this ghost stuff. In fact, I think he's the one who started the rumors about the break-ins."

Codey's eyebrow rose into a question mark.

The sheriff continued. "Yeah, the robberies are the reason I'm keeping my eyes open. A string of..." he paused and used to his fingers to produce air quotes, "a number of 'missing' items have been reported during the last few months."

Codey asked, "You think they were stolen, right? And not misplaced?"

The sheriff responded, "Nothing else makes sense. They're either stolen or it's some sort of prank. The gibberish floating around town claims ghosts are carrying off the missing goods into the great beyond."

"People actually believe that?" Codey asked.

"People believe what they want to believe. It doesn't help that when we investigated the crimes, there was no evidence of a break in, no windows were jimmied, no locks were picked, and not a single fingerprint left behind."

"The robbers had to be pros."

"That's what I am thinking. Several citizens reported missing items. Then later, they asked us to

60

forget the report was ever made. A few had the items returned, anonymously. Others wanted the investigation to stop."

"How is Sarge involved with this?" Codey asked.

"Sarge convinced every one of them their missing items were snatched up by spirits as payment for sins they committed in a previous life. He said they would be returned when their sins were paid for."

What a scam! Codey couldn't believe the Sheriff didn't see through it. He asked, "As in paid by cash payments made directly to Sarge?"

"As far as I know, no one ever paid Sarge a dime to get their items back."

"Did the disappearing goods happen to occur after Sarge had been in their house, looking for ghosts?"

The sheriff answered, "Sarge has worked his way into nearly every house and business in Deadwood. He's convinced the entire town is haunted. See, not all the whackos live in Chicago. We have a few here, as well."

Codey let the Sheriff's comment slide. He asked, "How valuable was the property taken?"

"Petty stuff, even house slippers were lifted. But there has been a string of robberies at Lame Johnny's that's baffling."

Codey's instinctive warning system activated inside of him. "The hotel my mom and I are staying at?"

The sheriff nodded. "Nothing of value. Seems more like the acts of kids, more than anything else, and a few of the items were returned, even a few wallets with money still in them."

"Speaking of Lame Johnny's, any news yet on Johnson's killer?"

"We're stringing a few facts together. There's a good chance we'll be able to make an arrest within the next few days."

"That's fast," Codey said, impressed.

"Well, it has to be fast, right? If it goes longer than 48 hours, the killers usually get away. I don't care what happens on those stupid TV shows, cold cases are rarely solved." The sheriff shook his head in disgust. "Those shows are wrong on so many levels."

Codey replied, "For one thing, cops don't eat donuts."

The Sheriff replied, "Nor do we shoot at a perp whenever we get a chance. Most of us have never fired a single shot during our entire career."

Codey nodded in understanding. The two men were bonding over stereotypes and misconceptions. His fellow law enforcement officer seemed to have forgiven him for stepping into the murder scene the night before.

The sheriff's mood shifted. Shooting Codey a crooked grin, he said, "And then there's Tillie ... well, you can probably figure out why I wanted to interview her."

Codey grimaced. He knew what was coming. It was the same rant he'd given his mom when she told him about her bus driver's background—a litany of reasons why she shouldn't have an ex-con connected in any way to Take A Chance Tours. The fact that Tillie once shot out the tires on a cop car was unforgiveable to him. He told his mom, "once a con, always a con", though he didn't actually believe that completely. People could change, but unfortunately they rarely did.

The sheriff continued, "I mean, unless you're interested. I figure, you wouldn't be considering your unfortunate situation."

"What unfortunate situation?" Codey asked, slightly ticked that his private life had been discussed in front of a sheriff. Plus, he was confused. He had no idea how his life could be considered unfortunate.

62

Buckley responded as if it were no big deal. He said, "That you'll be wearing a ball and chain soon. Tillie said you were engaged."

"How the heck did that come up in the conversation?" Codey blurted out.

Buckley laughed. "I was trying to see if Tillie belonged to you. I make it a rule to never take another cop's property."

"Property?" Codey questioned, the sheriff now beginning to get on his nerves.

Buckley grinned, "If you must know, I'm planning on asking Tillie out on a date."

EIGHT

Betty edged into the seat in front of a Whales of Cash penny machine. She needed to take a breather and might as well do it while sitting next to one of her clients. It had been a busy morning. The one-hour historical tour, thanks to Chuck's constant verbal intrusions, turned into a two-hour trek. By the time she returned to Lame Johnny's she needed a pick-me-up. A shot of espresso and a little game play would elevate her mood. She slipped a ten-dollar bill into the machine. At twenty cents a spin, the tenner should last a while. Betty never planned on winning. She only gambled with the money she could afford to lose. If she ever got to the point of playing with money to win money she'd lost, she'd stop—for good. She'd seen too many lives destroyed by the distorted reasoning that the only way out of gambling debt was to gamble more.

"How ya doing, Ester?" Betty asked. This was her client's second trip with Take a Chance.

"Pretty good. I've won over five hundred dollars since we arrived last night."

"That's great!"

"Well, of course, that's not counting the money I put into this machine."

Betty had run across this baffling form of accounting before from a dedicated gambler. It was a skewed form of rationalization that had their wagering always coming up in the black.

A cocktail waitress walked up, dressed like a western Saloon girl. She asked, "Care for a drink?"

"Can I have a shot of espresso?" Betty answered, tipping a dollar. The server would get another buck when she returned with the request.

"Want Kahlua in that?" the server suggested.

"Nah, just the caffeine," Betty responded.

Ester said, "I'll have a scotch on the rocks. Actually, make that a double."

The server walked away, scribbling on her notepad as she did.

Ester leaned in and said, "So, is it true what they're saying? That you know every lurid detail about the homicide last night?"

So much for a relaxing interlude.

Betty had to ask, "Who told you I did?"

"One of your riders, an older woman. I can't remember her name," she answered, and pulled a camel cigarette out of a bejeweled, gold plated case.

An older rider hardly narrowed it down. Betty took a chance. "Did her name happen to be Hannah?"

Ester nodded. "That's her. She mentioned it during breakfast."

Betty's face tightened. "How many other people were sitting with you at the time?"

"Well, we pulled a couple of tables together by that point. Probably six or seven."

By the end of the day, that number could easily morph into hundreds who heard Betty was an insider to a homicide. Gossiping was, after all, way cheaper than gambling.

Betty answered honestly, "I really don't know too much about it. Codey and I only went to the room where the incident occurred, and we did that after it happened."

"You mean your cop son? Isn't he on vacation? What's he doing checking out a crime scene?"

Betty wanted to respond that anyone in law enforcement was never actually on a holiday. Their acute social consciousness traveled with them. Betty answered, "He is. Both of us are letting the local sheriff handle any investigation."

"So that means you're not going to get involved with helping Chuck?"

Betty's ears perked up. "Chuck?"

"Yeah, you know the guy that likes yammering? Short, balding..."

"What happened to him?" Betty interrupted, her throat tightening at the possibilities.

"Didn't you hear? Chuck's wallet was stolen."

Betty relaxed. True one of her clients being robbed was disturbing, but that was bound to happen at one point or another. She said, "Even a small town has pickpockets, so I..."

Ester interrupted, "It wasn't a pickpocket. The wallet was stolen from his room. The scary thing is he doesn't who know took it, if it was a burglar or..."

"—a ghost." Betty finished the woman's sentence, which wasn't very hard to do. By now, half of the passengers would be agreeing with Tillie's obsession.

Betty stood up abruptly and handed a buck to the woman. She asked, "Would you mind giving this to the server when she gets back with my espresso?"

"Do you mind if I drink it?"

Betty shook her head no.

"Good," The woman said, before adding sheepishly, "the double scotch she's bringing me is my second for the day. And it isn't even noon."

Or high noon, Betty wanted to quip back. Instead she said, "Be my guest" before scurrying off to find her least favorite historian.

66

∞

Two establishments away from Lame Johnny's, Betty found Chuck seated at a two-dollar slot. Luckily, he responded to her text and mentioned where he was gaming. For a change, he didn't supply a plethora of details. That fact alone convinced Betty she needed to check up on her client in person.

Chuck was pressing the max bet button, which translated into six bucks a spin. He was both chortling and chatting non-stop to his slot neighbor whose face wore an expression of repressed annoyance. Within a minute, the neighbor left and Betty slid into his chair.

"Oh, hi!" Chuck said, acting surprised to see her, though she'd texted him fifteen minutes earlier.

"How are you?" She asked, generally concerned. Losing every bit of identification plus credits cards could be a catastrophe while on vacation.

Chuck shot back, "I'm great. In fact, I'm up one-hundred and sixty bucks."

Betty responded gently, "I wasn't talking about that. I meant, how do you feel after losing your wallet, ID, and your…"

This time it was Chuck who interrupted. "Oh, I didn't lose anything except the wallet. Not a single dollar or a shred of ID."

Betty said, "How could that happen?"

Chuck answered, "Every night when I walk into my hotel room, I empty out my wallet. Then I lock up my money, ID, and anything else inside the wallet in the safe."

Betty asked, "You empty it out every night?"

Chuck nodded. "Sure do. Then I set it on the nightstand next to the bed. I also toss my Rolex on the nightstand as well."

His actions made no sense to her, nor did it make sense that he didn't lock such a pricey watch in the safe. The timepiece was worth more than Betty's car.

She asked, "Why didn't you put your wallet into the safe? Along with your ID and money?"

Chuck answered, "Because, every morning when I put everything back into the wallet, I know exactly what I have on me. It's like taking a daily inventory of my cash. That way I'm sure I haven't lost anything of importance."

"So let me get this straight, an empty wallet was stolen? And whoever took that, didn't bother to take your Rolex?" Betty asked.

Chuck nodded his head.

Flustered, Betty continued, "And you're sure it's lost? That it didn't slip under the bed? Maybe fell into an open drawer?"

Chuck responded, "Security came up and looked for it with me. We spent a half-hour searching. They even looked in the tank at the back of the toilet."

Betty asked, "During the night, while you were in bed, did you hear anyone come into your room?"

"Nah, but I'm a heavy sleeper, plus I use a sleep machine. Once I plug that baby in, I can't hear a thing. And then, well, I had a three or four cocktails at the bar and..." He didn't bother to finish.

Chuck managed to score a Perfect trifecta when it came to increasing the odds of being robbed in your hotel room.

"Did you latch the door?" Betty asked, knowing that act alone wasn't a guarantee of security. There were too many YouTube videos floating around showing how easily a hotel door latch could be compromised.

"Probably," Chuck answered, hitting the play button again. Three mixed sevens appeared, awarding a forty-five-dollar win.

Chuck reached into his back pocket and pulled out a brown leather wallet stuffed with currency. He handed it to Betty.

"Neat isn't it? All the carving?"

Betty studied the hand-tooled engravings. The artisan depicted Bison roaming the rolling landscape of the Black Hills. She handed it back, stating, "It's absolutely lovely."

Chuck added, "Should be for the price. The one the burglar stole was a Velcro wallet. Had it since the eighties. It was falling apart, but I didn't want to get rid of it. I liked hearing the ripping sound when I opened it."

Suddenly, a thought occurred to Betty. Codey's birthday was only a few weeks away. "Where did you say you bought it? I might want to get one exactly like it for my son."

"Across the street at Harney's Jewelry & More."

Betty stood up to leave and said, "To be honest, I'm happy to see you're taking being robbed so well." Though Betty didn't know if that were the case, the empty wallet could still be somewhere in his room.

Chuck shrugged, "Well, it's not as if they got anything of actual value. So, I'm fine, except…" Chuck pressed the cash out button. "I'm not convinced it was a robber who broke into my room."

"Why not?"

He answered, "I realize I was completely wiped out, but you'd still think I'd notice someone standing right next to me."

Betty nodded in agreement, though if Chuck was inebriated as he alluded to being, he might not have been able to see or hear anything.

Chuck added, "I've been thinking. I mean, who would take an empty wallet? They had to be able to tell there was nothing in it by the weight alone. It doesn't make any sense."

"I agree," she added. "But maybe whoever it was, might have grabbed it and ran out as quickly as possible before checking the contents."

"Well, the way I look at it, is that they're either idiots," he said as he grabbed the paper voucher from his machine, "or dead people. Of course if I caught sight of them, I could tell you their history and where they…"

NINE

Tillie stood alone, in the center of the walk-in shower, the intense flow of water pellets stinging her naked curves. Her red hair piled high on her head, covered in bubbles and a flowery smelling shampoo. Scrounging around an hour earlier in the mud cellar left her feeling both grimy and confused.

Evan's attitude during their search of Harney's disturbed her. At every opportunity Evan ridiculed the thought of contacting the other world. Sarge seemed to take his comments well, but Tillie found herself irritated. She didn't think it common for a reporter to belittle his subjects, especially before he actually wrote the article. She was beginning to think that God blessed him with such good looks in order to compensate for his cynical personality.

Tillie decided, momentarily, to leave her concerns behind. There were few things she enjoyed more than indulging in a long hot shower. True, she was scheduled to meet Betty in a few minutes for lunch, but the scent of her shampoo was intoxicating, mesmerizing actually, and ... Wait a minute!

Tillie quickly rinsed out the remaining shampoo and turned off the shower. She grabbed the shampoo bottle from the wall rack and read the ingredients. She always used the same shampoo, even carried it with her on the tours. It was an Orange Blossom and Honey blend.

But that wasn't the fragrance that surrounded her. She was overcome with the smell of lavender. Tillie glanced down at the barely used mini bar of body soap, lifted it to her nose and inhaled deeply. Nothing. She stepped out of the glass enclosure and rushed toward the bathroom counter, nearly slipping on the wet marble floor.

A still unopened bar of hotel soap rested on the counter. It was the same brand in the shower. She studied the ingredients listed on the label. There was no mention of Lavender. In fact, the packaging proclaimed the soap to be scent-free, like the unopened bottles of hotel shampoos sitting next to it.

It was then, and only for a half-a-second, that Tillie saw what she would later claim were striking green eyes staring at her from inside the wall mirror, watching her every move. It could have been a reflection of herself she caught, distorted by steam and foggy glass. Instead, Tillie chose to believe she was not alone.

"Really? You followed me from Harney's?" She asked out loud in an irritated tone. "I understand it's lonely in your world, but taking a shower is kind of private."

Tillie wrapped a towel around her and left the bathroom, shaking her head at the ghostly intrusion on her privacy, as the hotel room phone rang. Her wet feet sunk into the thick carpet as she headed toward the nightstand.

"Hello," she said, fully expecting Betty to be on the other end, asking why she was late.

"Tillie McFinn?" the male voice asked. "This is Sheriff Buckley … Joe Buckley."

"What is it, Sheriff?" Tillie asked, her throat turning parched. It was hardly good when a Sheriff called your hotel room, or your house for that matter.

72

He stammered, "I was wondering if you had dinner plans for this evening?"

Tillie quickly realized the reason for the call. She plopped down on the bed. "Yeah," she answered coquettishly. "I plan on having dinner."

"That's not what I mean, I..."

Even over the phone, Tillie could tell the Sheriff was acting flustered, like a teenage boy asking the girl of his dreams to the prom.

Tillie decided to put him out of his torment. "I'm sorry Sheriff, but I already have plans to meet Betty. After that, I'm meeting Sarge and Evan to..."

The sheriff interrupted. "What about a midnight snack?"

"I have no idea how long we will be ghosting. If we run into a..."

The sheriff interrupted. "Then breakfast it is," and hung up the phone before Tillie would have responded with a No, it isn't.

Furious, Tillie scanned the room for any sign of her spirited intruder. She yelled, "See, what I have to put up with? Men! You should be happy you're a ghost."

And although it might have been coming though the walls from the room next door, the giggle Tillie heard made her shiver.

∞

At one p.m., the entrance to Blackie's Buffet was packed. Over twenty patrons waited in line, anxiously looking at their watches. The afternoon bingo session was only an hour away. A slot tournament featuring over ten thousand dollars in cash prizes was scheduled for the same time. Or perhaps those in the queue were

73

merely eager to start eating. The food at Blackie's was just that good.

Fortunately for Betty, she and Tillie were able to use the VIP entrance reserved for high rollers, invited quests or tour hosts. Within a matter of minutes, the two were seated at a table, exchanging conversation with their server.

"Would either of you like a beverage?" the young man asked, placing two tall glasses of ice water in front of them. His smile lit up a ten-foot area around him. His dark, swarthy looks suggested Lakota ancestry. His glistening long black hair was tied behind his neck with a thin leather strap. His nose was angular and his cheek bones high and defined. He asked, "Soda? Wine? Cocktail?"

"Iced tea," Betty answered.

"Me too," Tillie said dreamily, her face resting in her palm and her elbow was firmly planted on the table.

As soon as the waiter walked away Tillie lifted her head and asked, "Are all the men in the Dakotas gorgeous?"

"He is cute," Betty answered, her eyes scanning the various food stations. Cute men were not as interesting to her as the dessert of the day.

"Cute? The guy could win a beauty pageant and his runner-up would be Bradley Cooper. And he's not the only hunk, there's Evan, Sheriff Buckley, and..."

Tillie's comment about the law enforcement officer caught Betty's attention. It was the moment she'd been waiting for, a reason to know why the Sheriff escorted Tillie and her friends down the sidewalk.

Betty interrupted, "What did the Sheriff want with you this morning? Is there something I should be concerned about?"

"Not at all. It was no big deal, though he did insist we follow him to the police-station."

Betty replied, "That sounds like a big deal to me."

"He wanted to know where we would be doing our investigating and what our specific plans were for the weekend. He was pretty friendly, offered us coffee. Served us a batch of incredible sunflower seed oatmeal cookies."

Betty asked sarcastically, "Since when do cops haul people off the streets to serve them treats?"

Tillie answered, "Maybe it's a South Dakota tradition. He did ask if we'd gotten the permission from the owners of the property to search their premises."

Betty asked, "And did you?"

Tillie answered, "Sarge told him we had."

"Does that normally happen? Law enforcement questioning paranormal investigators like that?" Betty asked, doubting if Chicago cops would give a flying fig leaf about a trio of wannabe ghost busters.

Tillie shook her head. "The sheriff said that paranormal investigations in the Black Hills are becoming so popular, he's thinking about getting the city to require a license to do it."

"That seems a little odd," Betty remarked. She didn't add that if a municipal did require licensing, it would legitimize the occupation.

Tillie answered, "I thought so, too. I think he may have brought us to the station for a hidden agenda."

A flashback of another cop going berserk and trying to connect Tillie to a lethal crime flooded Betty's mind. She sucked in air and bolted upright before asking, "What?"

Tillie answered, "The sheriff called my room a few minutes ago. He wanted to know if I'd have dinner with him. When I told him no, he asked me out for a midnight snack. I told him no again and he insisted I meet him tomorrow for breakfast. He hung up before I could say no."

Betty relaxed, her shoulders losing their built-up tension. She said, "Tillie McFinn! Really? Another cop in love with you?"

Tillie took a sip of water before adding, "It's hardly love, more like lust gone wild."

Betty asked, "What did you say to him?"

Tillie shot her a wicked smile. "I'll tell you after I grab a plate of food."

The bus driver stood up and headed to the station marked BBQ. Betty watched as Tillie loaded her plate with ribs, pulled pork and grilled corn on the cob.

Betty decided to hit the salad bar. Huge chilled bowls of fresh organic spring greens sat next to smaller bowls of olives, grape tomatoes, chunks of blue cheese, chopped up scallions, fresh mushrooms, and more. Over thirty different edibles were offered. Once the food on her plate looked as if it might topple over the edge, she walked away, averting her eyes from the Bread Basket station.

Been there, done that, Betty reminded herself. She'd already had enough carbs for the entire day, and possibly for a year. Like a lot of women, Betty flip-flopped between low carb and high carb dieting, and every other diet in between. Basically, every morning she'd get up and ask the same question, "Which diet am I on today?" To keep her sanity, the answer was often none.

Tillie slid into the seat next to Betty. Her plate was a colorful accumulation of barbeque and carb-loaded sides. Tillie grabbed the small bowl of sunflower butter, and spread it over the already buttered grilled corn.

"So…?" Betty asked, expecting Tillie to fill her in on the details of her promises to the sheriff.

"I was going to say 'no way' but he hung up before I answered. "Tillie sprinkled salt over her mountain of food while Betty fought back resentment that her friend could eat anything and not gain an ounce. Tillie wouldn't even suffer bloat from the dump truck load of salt she'd poured.

"He's expecting to meet with you then?" Betty asked.

"Well, if he is, then he's going to be eating his bacon alone. Like I said earlier, I'm here on business," Tillie said before biting off a chunk of kernels from a corncob. "Besides, I don't want to attract too much attention while I'm with you. After all, I am representing Take A Chance Tours, as well as my chapter of G. H. U."

Betty couldn't help but smile. The non-attention getting outfit Tillie was wearing consisted of cream-colored spandex leggings, and a pastel blue embroidered eyelet off-the-shoulder crop top with flared sleeves. Dangling over her shoulder was a powder-blue, mini leather cross over bag. On Tillie's feet were her most prized possession, a pair of cream-colored Jimmy Choo high heel wedges she'd bought on clearance for ninety-five percent off of retail. A heck of a deal considering the full retail price was over six hundred dollars.

Betty said, "Speaking of the club, did your trio find any supernatural beings this morning?"

Tillie answered, "Well, we were only looking for ghosts, nothing else." The quizzical look Betty gave, forced Tillie to explain, "You know like demons, goblins or…"

Please don't say zombies, Betty prayed to herself, wondering how much of Tillie's vivid and exaggerated belief system she could handle.

"Or zombies," Tillie added, not noticing that Betty swore under her breath when she mentioned the Z word. "But yeah, I think I might have run into one. An upstairs gal from the 1800s hanging out in the basement of Harney's. We're going back this afternoon to search the attic."

"For more upstairs girls?"

Tillie shrugged. "More anything."

Betty saw her son loping across the room toward their table. Even if he wasn't her offspring, Betty had to admit he was a good-looking man.

"Hey Mom, Tillie," Codey said, sliding into the seat across from the two women.

Tillie blurted out, "Did I see you leaning on a building across from the police station?"

Codey looked embarrassed when he nodded yes.

"Were you following me?" Tillie asked, her tone light hearted, as if men following her was an everyday occurrence. It was.

"Yes," Codey mumbled.

Betty interjected, "I figured you were going to do that when you claimed you were leaving the historical tour to gamble."

Her son said, "I thought there might have been a problem I needed to be too aware of. Turns out, there wasn't."

This time it was Betty who folded her arms in front of her. She said, "I thought you and I were keeping our noses out of the sheriff's business?" Realizing how judgmental she must have sounded, Betty added, "Not that I wouldn't have done the same thing, if I could have."

Her son abruptly changed the subject. "How did the rest of the historical walk go?"

"Great. Actually, Chuck did most of the talking, so it was a piece of cake for me," Betty informed him. "We ended it at the Bullock Hotel."

Tillie chipped in, "The original owner Seth Bullock still walks the halls."

"The original owner is still alive?" Codey asked skeptically, his eyes wandering over to the food stations.

Tillie answered, "Nah, he died in 1919. But that doesn't mean he's still not getting in his daily constitutional. You would have liked him, by the way."

"Really?" Codey said in a tone that suggested Tillie had gone off her rocker for good.

Tillie replied, "He was a sheriff, you know a cop, like you."

Codey laughed and said, "Hardly."

Betty asked, "Are you going to grab some food?"

"For sure," Codey acknowledged, pushing back his chair slightly form the table. "If the server comes would you ask him to…"

"You mean ask my future boyfriend?" Tillie interrupted. Codey gave her a look that had her immediately explaining, "I have decided the waiter is so cute, he will be my beau after I run out of the boyfriends that I currently have."

Codey acted as if he didn't pay any attention to what Tillie had announced. He continued asking his mom, "Bring me coffee?"

"Sure," Betty answered, and then added, "But, while I'm thinking of it, did the sheriff verify the victim's name was Johnson?"

Codey said, "He did, but that wasn't too hard of a nut to crack."

"What do you mean?" Betty asked.

"One of the first things I noticed when we got to the room was the man's ID and money lying on the nightstand, right next to an ash tray with his snubbed-out cigar," Codey stated.

"I noticed that as well," Betty confessed before asking her most important question. "Did Buckley happen to mention if he found the man's wallet?"

"No," Codey answered. "I don't think he cares. The ID is the only thing that really matters. The man's cash and credit cards were still there, so robbery wasn't the motive."

Maybe not, Betty thought to herself. But, if Johnson's wallet was taken, the same thief may have taken Chuck's wallet. And, that same thief may have killed Johnson.

Betty swallowed hard. Her clients weren't safe after all.

TEN

At two p.m., the ruckus from the bingo hall spilled out into the hallway. The room was packed with raspy voices, coughs and cigarette smoke. Earlier, Betty purchased a fifty-dollar bingo packet. The game was not only fun, it allowed her to mingle with her clients. But, instead of playing, she decided to give a packet to the very next Take A Chance rider who showed up at the entry door.

Betty wasn't being generous. She basically didn't have the time for games, not when serious questions tugged at her. And one of those questions could only be answered by the woman who'd knocked into her the night before—the one who claimed her purse had been stolen from her hotel room.

Through the closed doors, Betty could hear the first Bingo number called. She took a glance at the stack of cards in her hand.

Darn it! B9! That number was clearly visible on the top card in her packet. It didn't help her mood when I-22 was called next.

Shoot! Two numbers in a row?

"It won't count if you hit bingo with those cards," Hannah's voice cut through her like a dull scalpel. "You have to be seated inside the hall to make it valid."

Crap! Of all the people to show up late to bingo, she hadn't expected it to be Hannah. Her passenger was a devoted player who always arrived early to set up a dozen miniature troll dolls around her bingo cards for luck.

"Hannah, you're never late. What's up?" Betty asked.

"I spent a half-hour searching for George Washington," Hannah answered glumly. Every single one of Hannah's trolls were named after presidents.

"You didn't find him?" Betty asked surprised, knowing Hannah protected her variety of talismans like a mother pit bull.

Hannah shook her head. "One minute he was sitting on the nightstand, and the next thing I knew George was missing in action."

A fearful tingle raced through Betty. This was the second item that disappeared from one of her clients.

Betty asked, "Did you check the floor? Or under the bed?"

Hannah snapped back, "Of course I did! GW was my very favorite troll. I won five hundred dollars the first time I set him next to my Bingo card."

"This could still be your lucky day after all, Hannah. This afternoon is on me." She handed the bingo packet to Hannah.

Hannah took the gift and stammered, "Really? Thanks!"

"You're welcome," Betty answered, and headed out of the hotel, hoping to find a little luck of her own.

∞

Standing next to the pull down steps that led into Harney's attic, Tillie gushed, "Sorry, I'm late." After lunch, she'd taken the time to change back in her ghost buster outfit, complete with the zipper testing cleavage.

Evan's eyes traveled slowly up and down her curves. He smiled before saying, "No problem." He held up a camera and snapped a few shots.

Tillie asked, "How much time did Old Man Harney give us?"

Evan released the strap held camera and let it rest against his chest.

"One hour," Sarge replied. "He doesn't want us bothering his tenants at night. That's why we have to do it now, before they get home."

The first floor of the building that housed Harney's Jewelry & More was retail and office space only. But half of the second floor had been converted into an apartment. The entrance to the attic was located directly outside the apartment door.

"More than enough time to find a spirit or two," Tillie answered.

Evan asked skeptically, "And why are we searching in broad daylight?"

Tillie answered, "Ghosts can appear anytime of the day. It's not like they have anywhere to go. And trust me, seeing a ghost in the daytime, will scare you a heck of a lot more than seeing it in the dark."

Sarge began his climb up the narrow steps and stepped into the attic. Evan motioned to Tillie to climb up the stairs.

Tillie responded, "Ah, no way cowboy. You go first. I'm not taking a chance that photos of my butt will be spread across your newspaper's website."

Evan laughed. "Damn woman, you read my mind." He shot her a wink and Tillie's heart fluttered. As Evan climbed the step, and she caught a glimpse of his muscular buns she immediately regretted her decision to be coy. Maybe Evan's having a snapshot of her ample derriere wouldn't be that bad. It would be something the two of them could laugh about with their grandkids, in fifty years or so.

As soon as Evan stepped into the attic, Tillie followed up the steps. Both men offered their hand to assist her into the vast, sweltering space. The rafters were low and Evan's hair rested against hanging cobwebs. The air was dense and Tillie realized they'd be lucky not to break into a sweat within the hour.

Cardboard boxes were tossed about on the floor, a few items of old clothing or tattered newspapers spilling out of them. A bookshelf leaned against the wall, a half dozen books rested on the shelf. Two sets of windows were directly opposite each other, on either end of the room. A few empty whiskey bottles were strewn about. A large wooden rat trap was set to catch a critter, but the dust on top indicated the trap had been set decades earlier.

Tillie walked over to a cheap, dented metal trunk. The top of the trunk was covered in dust. She opened the lid and nothing was in it except for a few ancient girlie magazines.

Evan was the first to mention the odor. "Man, that is the foulest cigar, ever. You think Old Man Harney could afford something better."

"If it is him," Sarge offered.

Evan snarled. "Who else could it be? It's not the tenants downstairs. They're both at work."

Tillie said, "Remember earlier this morning when we smelled flowers in the basement?"

Evan teased. "You mean the room freshener someone sprayed before we got there? That smell?"

Tillie didn't bother to respond to his jibe. Instead she said, "A female specter will emit a floral smell, but not a male. His smell is usually aftershave, tobacco or…"

"— Sweet grass if he's Native American," Sarge instructed.

"Right," Evan said in an unbelieving tone, and started snapping shots. He edged his way to the grimy

84

set of windows that looked out on Main Street. After taking a photo of the window, he checked his digital screen. "Jesus," he mumbled.

Tillie and Sarge rushed to his side.

"What is it?" Tillie asked, as she studied the window. Except for dirt, nothing was visible to the naked eye.

Sarge held out the camera for the two of them to look at his screen. He said, "It looks like..."

"A child 's handprints," Tillie interrupted, easily seeing the captured image. Yet, when she lifted her head and looked at the window directly nothing but dirt looked back at her.

Flustered, Evan said, "There has to be an explanation."

"There is," Tillie responded sadly. "It looks like a ghost kid, of around nine or ten years old was staring out the window, watching the living world go by."

Evan regained his composure and tossed in his cocky attitude. He said, "I'm sure when I download the images to my computer the smudges will not be there."

"Or maybe there'll be more," Sarge offered in return.

Tillie burst in, "Did you hear that? The bell?"

Evan admitted, "Yeah, actually this time I did. It could be coming from outside or from the shop below."

Sarge interrupted, "Tillie, do you think there are two ghosts hanging around here?"

"At least," she responded.

From the far end of the attic, suddenly a small wooden box fell off the bookshelf and slammed onto the floor. Startled, Sarge pulled his EFT thermal detector out of his backpack and clicked it on. Tillie didn't bother to remove hers. By the hairs standing up on her forearm, she already knew an entity was nearby.

85

Evan rushed to the bookcase. Tillie and Sarge followed.

Sarge studied his meter as he hustled across the rough, wooden floor. He mumbled, "The meter's spiking. We're not alone."

As soon as Evan reached the area, he took a few photos of the crashed box lying at his feet. He slowly panned his camera up to the shelves. Evan had clicked his camera into video mode. After he stopped filming, he picked up the small box and looked inside of it.

"That's an old recipe box," Tillie offered.

Evan answered. "There's nothing inside."

He placed the box back on the wooden shelves, took a few snaps, and then began to shake the rickety structure violently with his hands. Nothing happened. Moving the box closer to the edge, he shook again. And once again, he moved it toward the edge and shook. Eventually, the box tumbled off and fell to the floor.

"See," He said. "A rational reason—vibrations. A semi-truck must have driven by in the alley and shook the shelf."

"I didn't hear anything, " Tillie responded.

"Neither did I," Sarge added.

Tillie rambled, "And when you add the mysterious handprints…"

Evan interrupted, "Again, we don't know anything, not until I download the photos."

Tillie asked, "Sarge, do you want me to hold your detector so you can use your dowsing rods?" She pointed toward the thin, L-shaped brass rods hanging from his pant loop.

"Are we looking for water now?" Evan mocked.

Tillie offered, "The rods are used for many things. Like finding water, unmarked graves, or detecting the sex of a child. Trust me, it's very sciencey and objective."

Evan retorted, "Well, if it's sciencey, how can I doubt it?"

"Exactly," Tillie responded.

"By the way, dowsing rods are one of the oldest tools known to man," Sarge added, pulling the rods out and then pointing them outward as he slowly searched the perimeters around him. "Some people think they are advanced technology brought to earth by aliens."

Tillie read the look on the reporter's face. She asked, "Don't your eyes get tired, rolling around like that all the time? Your baby blues are beginning to resemble a spinning slot machine."

The man may have been a hunk, but he was obviously a born skeptic.

Evan smiled back. "So, you've noticed the color of my eyes?"

Tillie immediately turned her back on him. She didn't want him to see her blushing. She was so attracted to the man that it rattled her mind. Still there was something about him that also bothered her, but she didn't quite know what. Perhaps it was nothing more than his constant stream of cynicism.

And that is when she saw it, glimmering in the distance like rays of sunlight. She edged over to the corner and whispered, "Look."

The two men's eyes focused on where her fingers pointed.

A small gold nugget rested on the floor. Tillie picked it up and held it in her palm. She turned it over. The back was covered with a dark maroon colored substance.

"That's blood," Evan informed her. "Dried, old blood."

Evan's comments shocked her so that Tillie dropped the nugget accidently. It rolled along the rough wooden floor until it slid between two warped floorboards.

Tillie bent over to pick it up again and dropped it again in fright. This time it wasn't Evan's voice that scared her, but a stranger's.

A raspy voice from out of nowhere moaned loudly, "Bella! Come here!"

ELEVEN

By late afternoon Betty's pedometer registered over five thousand steps. For two hours she roamed Main Street looking for the nameless woman who'd bumped into her in the lobby the night before. The only rest stops Betty made were for a few sugared tidbits from the Squealing Squirrel, or to pick up tour tickets for her clients. Burned into her memory was the stranger's scowling face and sturdy-build. Before retreating to her room in defeat, Betty decided to check the neighboring hotel one more time, the same one the lady claimed she would be checking into.

The luxurious décor was a combination of an old time western saloon and Parisian brothel, a nod to the building's history. Overstuffed chaise lounges were upholstered in bright red silk with golden embroidery of peacocks. On the mahogany walls, lavish paintings hung next to rustic leather saddles. Dozens of small, framed mirrors were strategically placed throughout the area. Oriental carpet runners covered the walkways of the travertine tile floor. Tall ferns and deep green foliage completed the look. At the far end, the entrance to the gaming area beckoned with flashing lights, whoops of joy and moans of disappointment.

Betty headed towards the high-limit slot area. Instinctively, she knew the woman to be a high stakes gambler. For one thing, the heavy 18-karat gold chain around her neck rivaled any hip-hop artist's display of conspicuous wealth. Plus, the lady's French manicured fingers were covered in emerald and diamond rings. Eight rings in all, with a combined value worth more than Betty and Tillie's house put together. Considering the stranger's grumpy attitude, and the fact that she appeared to be traveling solo, Betty was also sure the woman only played slots, and her minimum bet would be twenty-five dollars a spin.

High-stakes slot players were a solitary lot who preferred sitting alone at a machine, sometimes for hours. The chatter and camaraderie around the game tables were too intrusive. Betty knew one woman who, except for occasional and rushed pee breaks, sat at a machine for twenty-four hours straight.

At the end of the high stakes slot room, was a private reception area for select players. Coffee was presented in silver urns, while white china cups and saucers rested on lace dollies. Trays of imported candied delicacies sat next to tins of imported jellies and miniature croissants. A few small tables and overstuffed chairs allowed high stakes players to take a momentary break from the action. Betty almost let out a yelp of joy when she finally saw the woman sipping cream laced coffee and popping a coconut-covered chocolate into her mouth.

Betty headed to the table. She said, "Excuse me, do you remember bumping into me at Lame Johnny's?" Betty didn't add the woman nearly knocked her to the ground.

"Oh no, don't tell me you're injured. You're not going to sue, are you?" The woman's voice took on a weary tone of 'Not again.'

Perhaps being wealthy had its drawbacks after all, Betty mused. The wealthy were always a target, one way or another, justified or not.

"I'm perfectly fine. My name is Betty Chance. I own Take A Chance Tours out of Chicago."

Sounding suspicious, the woman answered, "I'm Irene."

"I wanted to talk to you about your purse that is missing."

"Did you find it? I will gladly give you a reward..."

Betty shook her head. Irene's face slumped in disappointment and motioned for Betty to sit in the seat opposite her.

Betty asked, "So, no one's located it yet?"

"No, and it was a Michael Kors bag to boot."

"Ouch!" A Kors handbag was in the same stratosphere pricewise as Jimmy Choo shoes.

"Exactly," Irene responded.

Betty leaned in and said, "Do you mind if I ask, was there anything inside your bag when it went missing?"

"Nothing of value," Irene said, and set down her cup. "And that is why the whole thing is so strange."

"It is an expensive bag, so maybe the thief wants to sell it on eBay or Craig's …"

Irene held up her palm to stop Betty from speaking. She said, "It wasn't worth as much as what was lying next to it, forty-five one hundred dollar bills." Irene moved her wrist back and forth, causing her diamond bracelet to jiggle. "This was on the nightstand, as well."

Betty couldn't help but ask, "And are those diamonds?" She'd never seen as many diamonds in one piece of jewelry before, not on anyone she knew.

The look on the woman's face assured Betty she didn't know there was any alternative other than real. She didn't bother to answer.

Irene continued, "I was in the shower when the theft happened. I didn't hear anyone come in or out of my hotel room."

"Did you call security when you realized it was missing?"

Irene picked up a second chocolate-laced chocolate tidbit. "I did. And you want to know what security said as soon as I explained the situation?" She popped the bit of heaven in her mouth.

"Sure." Betty was curious. So far her experience with the security folks at Lame Johnny's hadn't been stellar.

Irene wiped her lips with a napkin. "The guy mumbled sarcastically, 'Bella's at it again'."

"Bella?"

Irene answered, "Lame Johnny's girlfriend."

"But that would mean, she's either 140 years old or..."

"—dead."

∞

Thirty minutes after hearing a strange voice from what she considered to be the beyond, Tillie sat alone with Evan at Johnny's Sister's Saloon. After the escapade in Harney's attic, Sarge retreated to his home, eager to update his blog with the latest paranormal discovery.

Evan pointed at Tillie's two giant frozen lime margaritas. He asked, "Are you sure you can manage all of that?" The din from slot machines lined along the walls, and a live country western band competed to be heard. The place was jammed with happy hour devotees.

"It's the perfect time to try," Tillie said, still shaken at the words mumbled in Harney's attic. "But, I only accepted the second one because it's free."

"I'm surprised hearing 'Bella, come here!' from a supposed ghost scared you as much as it did."

92

"Me?" Tillie responded, "You didn't exactly look like the man of steel when it happened."

Evan agreed, his cockeyed grin causing Tillie's estrogen level to resemble fireworks on the Fourth of July. "True, I did not, but neither did Sarge. I thought he was going to yell Mommy, help me, at any second."

"I think he may have," Tillie added. "To be honest, nothing like that has happened to me before."

Evan didn't look convinced. "I thought all of you ghost busters heard or saw ghosts on a regular basis."

"Oh, I've heard spirits. But their words were either hard to understand, or they came to me through the crackles of an EVP."

"EVP?"

Tillie took a short sip before answering, "That's the techy term for electronic voice phenomenon. It's kind of like a digital tape recorder for the dead."

"Another piece of research equipment you can buy on eBay, right?"

"I got mine on Amazon."

"Oh?" His tone suggested he still thought everything she and Sarge believed in bordered on the ridiculous.

Tillie responded honestly, "I'm surprised, after everything that's happened, you're not a believer."

Evan pulled his digital recorder out of this pocket and set it on the table. He powered it on to capture Tillie's words for his article. "Tillie McFinn, explain to me what you thought happened today."

Tillie answered, "Well, what did happen today was a wooden recipe box, which was sitting peacefully on a shelf, was knocked off by a spirit and landed on the floor."

"Go on," Evan instructed, leaning back in his chair as he placed his muscular arms behind his head. Tillie forced herself not to concentrate on the fact that his biceps looked like they would burst through the thin material at any minute.

Instead, she said, "After that, the same spirit led me to discover a blood soaked..."

"—Blood spattered," Evan corrected.

"Blood spattered gold nugget. According to the scale at Harney's, it weighed three ounces."

"Then what happened?"

Tillie was surprised she shivered as she recalled the incident. She said, "The words 'Bella! Come here!' filled the air."

Evan clicked off his recorder. Tillie reached over and clicked it on again.

Tillie demanded, "Now, Evan Rogers, tell me what you think happened." Even the reporter's smirk appeared sexy to her.

Evan answered, "The box was shaken loose by a vibration of some sort, perhaps a truck passing by, or the building's aging foundation settled. After that, you were lucky enough to see a gold..."

"—Blood splattered," Tillie corrected.

"Blood spattered gold nugget gleaming between two floor boards. It may have been there for decades or a hundred years. I'm pretty sure it was wedged between a floorboard or a joist, and was set loose by the same vibrations that sent the wooden box flying. Or maybe it even rolled out of the recipe box and we didn't notice."

"And then...?"

Evan laughed. "Well, that's where my logic turns a little fuzzy. Unless you or Sarge are a ventriloquist, I have no idea who or what called out for Bella."

Tillie sipped through the tiny straw, swallowed and teased, "Is it because the left side of your brain cannot accept what the right side of your brain is hearing?"

Evan's brow furrowed in confusion as Tillie sucked down the last of the liquid.

94

She said, "Don't you know that the right side of your brain handles all things creative and spiritual, while the left-side tackles things like math and being able to figure out what goes where. You're a left-brain thinker. Me? I'm totally right-brained."

Evan sat back down in his chair. He reached over and lightly touched Tillie's hand with his fingers. He playfully drew a circle on it, causing her estrogen to go on a high-speed ride through her body. He asked, "So what you're implying is that if we put our two heads together, we get one?"

Tillie laughed, wondering where his question was leading.

He playfully added, "And if we put out two bodies together…?"

That's where it's leading! Two bodies joining together was a scenario Tillie could not fantasize about for a second. If she did, the only ghosts she'd find that weekend would have to be galloping around under the sheets in the bed that she and Evan would never, ever leave.

Changing the topic of conversation would be the best thing to do at the moment. Tillie pulled her hand out of touching distance and said, "You must love being a reporter. It sounds so exciting."

Evan's expression turned granite. He responded in barely repressed anger. "Not anymore. At one time maybe, but with all the changes in the industry…"

Tillie regretted pulling her hand away from him. The man needed comforting. She asked, "Is it true that a lot of print newspapers are shutting down, one after another?"

"Or going to online versions that are ninety percent written by freelancers."

"Like the Dakota Daily?" She asked.

"Plus the money sucks. A guy can barely make a liv…"

He didn't bother to finish his sentence. Tillie didn't need for him to explain what he meant. Complaints of falling salaries in journalism, and lack of employment for new grads, were constant topics of conversations on talk radio.

She decided again to change the discussion. So far she was batting zero. Stirring her drink, she asked "Have you heard anything more about the murder?"

Evan threw back a fourth of his beer, and said. "Not really. I do know the sheriff asked Wyoming to hang around town."

"The escort?" Tillie inquired.

Evan nodded.

"Does he think she's..." Tillie didn't finish. It wouldn't be fair to Wyoming to connect her name to the crime. Tillie had suffered the result of false accusations in her past, no way would she allow that same pain to happen to anyone else.

Evan answered, "I have no idea what he thinks, but it's probably standard procedure. Deadwood may be small as compared to Chicago, but the law enforcement here is well trained.

"Like any gambling town," Tillie added. She'd heard too many complaints that when legalized gambling moved into a small town, so did big city crime.

She asked, "What's this sheriff like?" The only thing she knew about him was that he wouldn't take no for an answer.

Evan replied, "Buckley? He's an okay guy, I guess. Sarge told me he's turned into a skirt chaser since his divorce."

Tillie realized she was one in a long line of women the man had pursued. "Well it's a good thing I wear pants instead of skirts."

Evan smiled and Tillie melted into her chair. He said, "Yeah, but even pants have to come off,

96

sometime or another. Or at least, I like to think they do."

Tillie's face grew warm. If she didn't walk away from Evan now, she'd never have the courage to leave. She picked up the second margarita. Holding it firmly in her hands she lied, "I have to go. My boss is expecting me."

Tillie fled the bar, managing to not let a single drop of the cocktail leap out of the glass. A miracle actually when considering how much she'd managed to wiggle her hips in flight.

TWELVE

Betty waited patiently in front of the concierge desk at Lame Johnny's. She'd managed to secure twelve tickets for a local tour that included visiting Calamity Jane's grave and panning for gold. A dozen of her riders expressed interest in taking their chance at prospecting. After two days of gambling, they may have decided finding a fortune at the bottom of a pan was better odds than playing three-card poker. But, handing out the tickets would be problematic. Her clients were scattered across town. The only way she could make sure they'd receive them in time was to leave messages that the tickets would be held by the concierge. A twenty-dollar bill slipped into his waiting palm should make that happen.

She smiled warmly at the man behind the desk. "You don't mind doing this?"

"Not at all," the thirty-some year-old responded, sliding the folded bill into his pocket.

Betty caught his name on his brass nametag. She asked, "Chad, are you related to the Harneys who own…"

Chad finished her question for her. "—The store across the street? Old Man Harney is my grandfather." Chad must have read the uncomfortable look on her face. He added, "That's what everyone calls him. He's been around forever."

Betty couldn't tell by the tone of the man's voice if that was a good thing or not. He certainly didn't express any familial warmth in his tone. Maybe he was counting his days until a potential inheritance would allow him to leave the hospitality service far behind. He certainly wasn't very good at it. He'd grabbed the twenty like an alligator waiting to be fed.

As long as they were having a somewhat civil conversation, Betty decided to ask a few questions. "I have a client who had his wallet taken from him."

Chad said, "Chuck Fletcher. Security is still talking about him. Seems like he's more knowledgeable about Lame Johnny than any guest they've met."

Betty smiled back. "Do they have a lead … who might have taken it?"

Chad answered, "We're not investigating the disappearance."

Betty asked, "We're? By that you mean the hotel?"

Chad bristled at her comment. He answered, "I'm not the concierge, I'm the manager. It's a small hotel. We all chip in wherever we're needed."

"Oh," Betty replied, surprised at the man's stern insistence that he was more than he appeared to be.

Chad added gruffly, "Fletcher said the wallet wasn't of any value, and when he explained his situation the night before…"

Ah, the night before when Chuck was as drunk as a historian skunk.

Betty continued. "But haven't there been a few more incidents? Missing purses and wallets?"

Chad shifted uncomfortably on his feet. He looked around the room before stating, "Mrs. Chance…"

"—Ms. Chance," Betty interrupted. The word Mrs. still left a bad taste in her mouth. It reminded her of her one time cheating husband and his new sugar momma of a wife.

Chad continued, "I really shouldn't talk to you about any of this."

He gathered up the few papers that were lying on his desk, and abruptly walked away.

I hope that Grandpa's inheritance is big because odds are, you'll probably be fired someday, Betty wanted to yell. Instead, she headed toward the elevators. The moment she pressed the up button a familiar voice rankled her calm.

Sliding up next to her, Hannah said, "I didn't win a single bingo with that packet you gave me. Not a dollar."

Well, it's not like you paid anything for it. Betty said, "I'm sorry, Hannah."

Hannah shrugged. "That's okay, it's not your fault I didn't win a jackpot."

Betty was confused, not by the words Hannah was uttering, but by the fact her client wasn't blaming her for her misfortune. On every tour Hannah claimed Betty's actions cost her at least one jackpot, if not more.

Hannah continued, "You want to know whose fault it is?"

"Sure."

"The goblin who took my George Washington troll doll, that's who," Hannah said as the two women stepped into the elevator.

Betty decided to let Hannah's comments ride. Who was she to say there were no such things as goblins, especially if Hannah placed the blame on them instead of her?

Betty answered, "Maybe the culprit will decide to bring George back."

"He'd better," Hannah responded. "I paid two dollars and ninety-eight cents for that doll."

As the brass door opened Betty said, "It could always be a female ghost, you know like Casper's unfriendly sister?"

"No it isn't," Hannah answered. "I smelled the cigar smoke. One thing I know for sure, it was definitely male, and a frickin' pervert to boot." Hannah exited the elevator and began her trot down the hallway.

"And why is that?" Betty yelled after her.

Over her shoulder Hannah said, "Because I was taking a bath when he took it from the nightstand."

After all, when the troll was taken Hannah wasn't in the same room. For the first time, Betty realized the doll wasn't merely misplaced. George Washington was taken hostage.

∞

As soon as Betty walked into her hotel room, a blast of cold air rushed past her face. She refused to acknowledge it, like she refused to notice the floral scent that invaded her nostrils. There was a logical explanation for everything, she reminded herself of the sudden outburst of Ghostbusters music the night before? The words "who ya gonna call?" frightened her until she discovered Tillie had downloaded it on her iPod without her knowledge.

Tossing her purse on the bed, Betty sat down at the small table and turned on her laptop. Within a few seconds she was writing her daily blog posting.

"It is our second day in Deadwood! Our stomachs are full from the delicious food at Blackie's Buffet. I'm hoping the chef will give me the recipe for Cowboy Chili. If he does, I'll pass it along. So far on this tour, the gambling for many has been as appetizing as the food. One passenger won thirteen hundred dollars on "The Walking Dead" slot machine. A few of my riders will be trying their luck panning for gold tomorrow. I will let you know if they find a nugget or two."

Betty glanced down at the comments on her blog and her eyes immediately landed on Hannah's posted comment concerning the whirlpool murder where 'Betty was at the crime scene, as usual.' So far, none of Betty's readers had commented on Hannah's post. By now, perhaps even they knew what Hannah was like and didn't bother to respond.

Of course Betty could always remove Hannah's comments. But, if she did, eventually she'd have to deal with Hannah's version of hell to pay. Besides, Betty was a firm believer in free speech; even if it was Hannah doing the speaking, or in this case, posting. Betty's best bet would be to ignore it for now, everyone else seemed to be.

She posed her fingers to begin typing again when a rapping sounded, followed by the word "Betty?"

Within a matter of minutes, Tillie was sitting on the hotel bed in her room, carefully balancing a gigantic margarita in one hand. She held it outwards and said, "This is for you. I haven't taken a zip, I mean sip."

Betty's eyebrows arched into an I doubt that sort of look. She said, "Actually, you sound like you've been zipping for a while."

Tillie answered, "It was happy hour, so the drinks were two for one. I saved the second one for you."

"A bit much for you, isn't it?" Betty was not used to seeing Tillie intoxicated. Betty took the drink and set it on the table next to her. It looked tempting, but she had work to do.

Tillie said, "Not if you had the day I've had, it isn't."

"What happened? Did you find a ghost?"

"I'm afraid we did—emphasis on the word afraid."

"Really? You're afraid? I thought you lived for that stuff," Betty decided one little taste wouldn't hurt her. She held up the margarita and put the straw to her lips.

Tillie answered, "Oh, I definitely get frightened. That's part of the fun. I'm not used to it being so real that I'm terrified to the bone."

Betty asked, "What do you mean being so real?"

"Usually I see a vaporous form or hear a muffled word or two. But this time, it was as if the ghost was standing next to me, well actually over me. I heard every word he uttered as clearly as I hear you."

"What did he say?" Betty asked, not really buying into Tillie's story.

Tillie tried on a man's deep voice and said, "Bella! Come here!"

Betty's stomach did a somersault at the word Bella. It wasn't the first time she'd heard that name today.

Tillie continued, "Plus, I happened to be bent over at the time picking a gold nugget off the floor. I think he might have mistaken my rump for Bella's."

Betty asked, "Wait a minute … what gold nugget?"

Tillie answered as if it were no big deal. "The one I found in Harney's attic. Of course it belongs to Harney because we found it in his building."

"He had no idea it was there?" Betty asked.

"He said he didn't."

"Did he act surprised?"

"Not really. The first thing he did was weigh it on his jewelry scale, told us that it was worth thirty-six hundred bucks and then tossed it into his pocket like it was a stick of gum. He didn't even say thanks."

"He didn't give you a reward?"

103

Tillie shook her head. "Not even a discount coupon to his store."

The old man sounded incredibly cheap and grumpy. And if Betty had correctly detected any love lost between Chad and his grandfather, there may have well been a good reason for it.

Betty asked, "Did Evan and Sarge hear the words?"

"They did. Unfortunately, Evan didn't have his recorder turned on, but he did take a few shots of a child's handprints on the window and..."

Betty interrupted. "—I assume handprints of a ghostly nature, so yeah. You did have a busy day."

"And so are you," Tillie pointed at the margarita glass in Betty's hands.

Betty looked down. Without even realizing it, she'd drunk half the contents in a matter of minutes. She leaned forward, as if sharing secrets with her best friend. She said, "This isn't the first time today I've heard the name Bella."

Tillie's eyes popped. "Don't tell me your ghost mistook your rump for hers, as well?"

Betty responded firmly, "This hotel room is not haunted. I am the only occupant."

"Sorry to say this, but I totally disagree," Tillie responded. "Something is going on in this entire building."

Betty said, "I agree, but I don't think it's supernatural. Do you remember I mentioned a woman brushed into me in the lobby the first night we were here?"

Tillie answered, "Sure, the one that was checking out because the hotel is haunted, though you keep saying it isn't."

Betty nodded. "I searched her out today to ask her a question. She mentioned her purse was taken from her room and I wanted to know..."

104

Tillie interrupted, "—if it was empty like Chuck's wallet?"

"It wasn't, but nothing too valuable was inside. However, forty-five hundred bucks was lying next to it when it went missing, plus a diamond bracelet was left on the nightstand."

Tillie smiled broadly. "See? I'm getting good at knowing what to ask. You're rubbing off on me. Someday I will be an amateur sleuth like you.

Betty reminded her, "I am not an amateur sleuth."

Tillie shrugged. "Okay, sleuth enthusiast, whatever. Didn't you also say that Johnson's ID was lying on the table?"

"I did," Betty answered, already knowing where Tillie's train of thought was heading.

"You're thinking someone may have stolen his wallet?"

"I am."

Tillie continued, "And that same person could be not only an accessory loving thief but possibly a murderer."

Betty nodded. "But here's a question I'd like you to answer. Though to be honest, I do not think it to be in the realm of possibilities but…"

Tillie interrupted again, "Could a ghost snatch an item up and carry it away?"

"Yes."

Tillie answered simply, "Not only is it possible, it happens all of the time. Especially in the Black Hills."

Betty picked her drink up again. This time Betty didn't stop zipping, not until it was completely gone.

∞

Codey slowed his pace down as he passed by the Mt. Moriah cemetery. He gave a quick salute to Wild Bill Hickok's dirt home and continued his five-mile run circling the town. He'd be back in time take a shower and meet his mother for dinner; if she'd sit with him that is.

Betty insisted he set out on his own, start enjoying his vacation and 'let her be'. His mom reiterated she was safe, and so were her clients. Codey still wasn't sure. The tales of missing items, plus Johnson's murder set his police antennae on high alert.

Okay, he reminded himself. Focus on running and relax. Breathe in, breathe…

Yet, as soon as Codey turned the corner, his body tensed and he stopped abruptly. Lying on the road was a shredded, mangled body of a pioneer woman. Standing over the destruction was a vicious, snarling face that suggested Codey get the hell away.

Codey reached out his hand slowly, his palm held upward in peace. He whispered, "Hey girl, settle down. You okay?"

The chocolate Lab instantly turned from a fang-bearing ruffian into a panting cuddle bunny. She jumped over the fabric toy doll and onto Codey's torso. The tough Chicago cop patted the dog's head and leaned over asking, "Who's your daddy? Who's your Daddy?"

"I'm hoping you are," a female voice came from behind him.

If Codey could have blushed, he would have. He never showed his tender side in public, especially to a woman. But when Codey was around a dog, or a cat, he changed from a two-hundred-pound man into a ten-year-old whimpering girl.

The twenty-some-year old woman asked, "You're not, are you?"

The lab raced over to the woman and began to lick whatever was convenient and close.

Codey answered, "No, but's she's a great dog." The lab scurried to what was left of her toy, retrieved it and dropped it at Codey's feet.

The woman held out her hand for Codey to shake. "I'm Tiffany. I found her this morning, a few miles outside of town, looking hungry and thirsty."

Codey asked, "She didn't have any tags?"

Tiffany shook her head slowly, "None."

Codey noticed a stack of flyers the woman held in her hands. The word "Found" was printed in a 98-point font right next to a snapshot of the enthusiastic doll-destroying dog.

Tiffany asked, "You're a cop, aren't you?"

Was it that obvious? "Yeah," he answered.

Tiffany continued, "I saw you with my dad this morning. I was dropping off another tray of cookies. Dad likes to treat his suspects before tossing them into the slammer for eternity."

Codey's didn't know if she was kidding or not, and his expression must have shown it.

Tiffany grinned. "Well, not forever."

"The sheriff's your dad?" Codey asked.

Tiffany nodded. "You're staying at Lame Johnny's right, with your mom?"

Codey tried not to grimace. As soon as he left town the Legend of Mama's Boy Codey Chance was bound to live on through the centuries. It would be right up there with tales of Calamity Jane and Seth Bullock.

He mumbled, "Yeah, I am."

Tiffany continued, "Well, if I don't find the owner by the time you check out, maybe I'll let you arrest this charmer and take her back to the Windy City."

Actually, Codey thought, that would be nice, but he was wise enough not to tell that to Tiffany. He had a feeling she wasn't kidding.

107

Codey asked, "Do you know her name?"

Tiffany shook her head, "I've tried a bazillion names, and she didn't respond to any of them."

He patted the Lab one more time who then treated Codey's attention as if it were the best thing in the world–ever! The dog bounced her body up and down in delight while her panting went into hyper drive. Codey said, "I've got to get back. Good luck in finding the owner."

"Thanks," the woman yelled after him, holding back the lab to keep the dog from joining Codey in his run.

Codey lifted his hand in acknowledgement of the woman's comment. He upped his pace, heading back to the hotel, wondering why anyone would discard such a beautiful loving animal. It didn't make any sense, but then it never did. Maybe Deadwood wasn't the totally friendly and fun-loving town it appeared to be, after all. Maybe like every other place in the world, it too had a dark side.

THIRTEEN

The fact that Wyoming Nevada was mindlessly playing a penny slot baffled Betty. It was the first time she'd seen the young woman since the grisly scene in Johnson's room. Fighting against common sense, she decided to find out why Wyoming was still hanging around the hotel. Betty glanced at her watch. She was scheduled to meet Tillie at the buffet for dinner. She'd make her conversation as brief as possible.

Betty slid into the seat next to the escort and said, "Wyoming? Do you remember me?"

Wyoming turned toward Betty, her face deadpan. Betty noticed how different the woman appeared. Without make-up, and thick, false eyelashes, she looked years younger. Her bleached hair was pulled back into a ponytail, held by a hair-damaging rubber band. Her ear lobes were earring free and the four tiny little holes pierced into each lobe looked lonely for attention. Her face appeared haggard and her expression distant.

A light of recognition finally came into her eyes. Wyoming mumbled, "Oh, hi."

Betty asked sincerely, "How are you?"

Wyoming answered, "Okay, I guess." She slid a five-dollar bill into the machine and pressed play at twenty cents a spin.

Betty placed a twenty into her slot. It was a way to keep up the pretense that she just happened to sit down. She said, "That was pretty tough, the other night."

Sounding bitter Wyoming responded, "I've been through worse."

Her response wasn't a surprise. An escort's life wasn't usually a pretty one. Rainbows and unicorns were things of the past.

Betty asked, "Has the sheriff told you anything about the case? If he suspects someone?"

"Ha!" Wyoming scoffed. "I think I'm his number one suspect."

Of course, that made perfect sense. In the sheriff's eyes, who else would have a motive?

"Why do you think that?" Betty asked, forcing her tone to sound surprised.

Wyoming answered, "Because the Sheriff told me not to leave town. How stupid is that?"

"Pretty stupid, "Betty replied, though she would have done the same thing if she were Buckley.

Wyoming said, "Yeah, that's what I thought. It's not like I did anything wrong. I mean I did something right. Right? I notified the front desk the man was dead."

"Right, "Betty responded. "Are you staying at the hotel?"

"Yeah, a friend works here. I could stay at their place, but there's these nasty dogs and..."

Betty nodded in agreement while inwardly checking off not an animal lover on Wyoming's list of personality traits.

Wyoming continued, "Considering everything I've done for..." The young woman stopped talking mid-sentence, perhaps realizing she'd already said enough.

Betty wondered if the 'friend' was actually her 'john'. It may have been true Wyoming's first contact with Johnson was online, but the initial contact may actually have come through Wyoming's buddy. Someone who recognized a moneymaking opportunity when he saw it, like a man checking into a hotel alone.

Betty reached into her purse and pulled out a business card. She said, "My cell phone is listed. Please feel free to call me at any time of the day or night, if you need any help or want someone to listen."

Wyoming's shoulders dropped while her body relaxed. She took the card staring at it for a few moments before responding, "Thanks, maybe I will."

∞

By the time Betty met Tillie at the buffet entrance she was twenty minutes late.

"Sorry, something came up," Betty explained, but didn't mention Wyoming was the reason for her tardiness. "You should have started without me."

Tillie answered, "Nah, I figured I'd wait and let you know Codey's inside holding a table for us."

"Really? He promised me he'd take the night off," Betty said.

Tillie chuckled and asked. "From being your bodyguard or being your doting son?"

"At this time, both," Betty answered, as she and Tillie zipped through the VIP line.

Tillie pointed her index finger and said, "Well, if anyone will make him decide to give up his role as protector and run back to Chicago..."

Tillie didn't need to explain her comment any further. Hannah was standing next to Codey, chattering away as he toyed with the salad on his plate.

111

As soon as Betty was within earshot Hannah yelped loudly, "Your poor son has been sitting all alone. It's like he's an orphan."

Betty answered, "Well, he did have you to..."

Hannah interrupted. "And it's a good thing I am here. Did you know he was about to add a heaping tablespoon of sugar to his coffee? I told him half the people in this buffet have diabetes because they used to do the same."

Betty mumbled, "Thank you," while restraining herself from bursting out into laughter. Not too many women who weighed less than a butterfly were brave enough to confront a 6' 2" burly cop about his eating habits.

Hannah said, "I've never once let my son the lawyer eat white poison in front of me..." She paused before adding reluctantly, "though he does tend to drink a lot, now."

You think?

Although she didn't want to, Betty did the only polite thing to do. She asked, "Hannah would you care to join us?"

Hannah responded, "No thanks. I'm having dinner with Jerome. You know, the guy that cheats at Roadside Bingo? Calls out bison when we're not even playing?"

Betty's ears perked up. Jerome? Was Hannah going on a date?

Hannah continued, "I only stopped by to save your son from digesting poison and to tell you something, if you ever showed up, that is."

"What?"

Hannah announced, "I found George Washington."

"Who?" Codey asked.

Hannah answered, "GW, my lucky troll doll."

"Ah," Codey replied.

Betty asked, "Where was he?"

"How would I know? It's not like he told me," Hannah answered.

Betty asked, "I mean, where did you find him?"

Hannah said, "Like I told you earlier, someone stole him. When I returned to my room after bingo he was propped up on my pillow like he was Bill Clinton."

"Well, that's wonderful news, so…"

"No it isn't. His little body is riddled with punctures, like someone was trying to tear him apart with their teeth."

Betty watched as Hannah walked towards Jerome who beamed a smile as he noticed her coming his way.

Betty sat down across from Codey and said, "Hannah's troll dolls are talismans she uses religiously while playing bingo."

"I guessed that," her son answered.

Tillie piped in, "I prefer four leaf clovers and leprechauns."

Codey said, "Which you undoubtedly believe work."

"Totally," Tillie answered. "The proof is in the pudding - winning."

Codey asked, "Did someone pickpocket our first President during Hannah's bingo game?"

Betty shook her head. "No, from her room. She claimed it was sitting on the night stand."

Tillie asked, "And then suddenly it was gone?"

Betty nodded.

"Like Chuck's wallet," Codey said, his voice taking on an investigative tone.

"Exactly," Betty answered. "Irene's purse was also taken while she…"

Codey interrupted. "—I don't remember an Irene on the bus." He folded his arms in front of him and said, "Mom, you're not talking about the woman who bumped into you the first night we were here, are you?

113

The one who claimed her purse had been stolen? And the hotel haunted?"

Instead of responding, Betty took a long sip of water, hoping to put off the inevitable mother son confrontation.

Codey continued, "Funny, but I don't remember that woman sharing her name with us."

Betty gave a weak smile, as if it were no big deal. Her tactic didn't work. Codey didn't release his pose.

Through gritted teeth he asked, "Mom, don't tell me you tracked her down?"

Betty mumbled, "Would you believe me if I told you I bumped into her?"

"I would not, "Codey answered firmly.

Betty decided it would be a good time to flee to the food station. She lifted herself up and said, "Well, maybe I'll grab some food. I hear tonight's special is really…"

"Mom?" Codey demanded.

Betty plopped back into the chair.

Codey said, "Well, I guess I should ask…did you find anything out at all? And if you did, tell me what you found out, no matter how minor it is. I don't want to spend my night worrying you discovered something that will put you in danger."

Betty answered, "Nothing really, except Irene's purse was basically empty when it was taken."

"Like Chuck's wallet?" he asked. "And like Hannah's troll doll, it had no actual value, then?"

Betty said, "I wouldn't say no value. It was a Michael Kors bag."

"Cha ching!" Tillie responded. She looked at Codey's confused face. "Trust me, it's worth a ton of money. You can't buy a Kors at The Dollar Tree."

Betty continued, "But what's odd is she claims forty-five hundred dollars in cash was sitting next to it.

Plus, her diamond bracelet was in full-sight on the nightstand."

Tillie said, "So, I guess the robberies aren't about money."

Codey answered, "It's always about the money."

"Always?" Tillie asked.

Codey relented. "Well, almost always. But if it's not, then it's about…"

Betty answered for him. "—Power."

∞

The elevator doors slid open and Betty stepped out into the middle of the second floor hallway. She turned left and walked slowly toward the end, scanning the perimeters, trying to catch a glimpse of a security camera. Surveillance equipment had evolved to the point where a camera could easily be the size of a dime. Reaching the end, she turned and headed back in the opposite direction. Once she checked the entire floor she'd do the same thing on the third floor. Then from the top level she'd walk down the emergency stairwell, checking out every square inch.

As far as she could tell, there wasn't surveillance on any of the upper levels of the hotel. Like many of the smaller gaming resorts, the owners only bothered to install cameras on gaming floors or in the lobby. Someone could easily break into a room at Lame Johnny's undetected. And, unlike many of the casinos she's stayed at, Betty didn't have a close connection with anyone in security who would answer her questions. Take a Chance Tours had only stayed at this particular hotel once before, and it had changed ownership since then. Betty was good with remembering faces and not a single one of the current employees looked familiar to her.

Of course if she found a hidden cam, she had no idea what she would do with the information. Tell the Sheriff? He probably already knew. Ask him why Johnson's assailant wasn't captured on tape walking down the hallway? And why wasn't he, or she, arrested yet?

But Betty wasn't only searching for information about the murder. This was the second Take A Chance rider who claimed an item was taken from their room. Though, it would be easy to discount Hannah's ramblings as a senior who merely misplaced something, the woman couldn't be written off that easily. Not when it came to her troll dolls. She protected them like a machete-wielding mother bear defending her cubs.

The door to the service elevator slid open. Betty watched a young maid push a service cart down the hallway filled with freshly folded linens, bars of soaps, and other toiletries. Her tight fitting uniform revealed every curve, hill and valley. If Tillie's Evan looked like Kevin Costner, this woman was South Dakota's version of Charlize Theron.

The employee stopped in front of a room but didn't bother to knock. She unlocked the door and entered. The room was unoccupied and in the process of being prepared for the next occupant.

Betty rushed to the doorway and said loudly, "Hello?"

The employee walked out of the bathroom, her hands filled with a stack of crumpled, white towels. "Can I help you?"

Betty asked, "Could I take a gander at this suite? I'd like to recommend it to my clients. I run a tour company."

"You bet," the woman answered and turned around and headed back into the bathroom.

Betty entered the room and rushed toward the balcony. She wasn't interested in familiarizing herself with anything except the access the balcony provided. She slid the sliding glass door open and stepped out on the wooden deck.

The balcony was one long continual structure that ran along the front of the building. The only privacy from one room to the next were strategically placed flowerpots, with tall snapdragons growing. The City of Deadwood positioned live webcams on Main Street, but she doubted if the cams would include images of Lame Johnny's. The cameras were too far away.

A person could have exited the suite next door onto the balcony, pushed aside the flowerpots, and entered the room through the sliding patio doors, undetected. Of course that would mean the culprit would have had to have a way to get into an adjoining room, or was even staying in it.

Betty stood on the deck, staring up at the roof and decided there was another option. Chuck and the dead guy's suite were on the third floor. Someone could easily climb down from the roof with the help of a rope ladder. The only problem with that theory was that Hannah's room was on the second floor.

The maid called out to her. "Are you finished looking around?"

Betty stepped back into the room, and closed the sliding door behind her.

"Yes, thank you, "Betty said and handed the woman a five-dollar tip for her cooperation. "Can I ask you a question…?" Betty paused to read her nametag, "Sasha, have any of the hotel guests mentioned the rooms are haunted?"

She laughed. "About a million of them. I can tell you one thing, if they don't believe in ghosts when they check in, they usually believe when they check out."

"That's kind of scary," Betty said.

Sasha answered, "I don't know if it's scary but it's certainly good for business, if you know what I mean."

Betty said bluntly, "I don't. Tell me." She slipped the employee another five.

Sasha leaned into and whispered, "Since the new owner took over, rumors of Lame Johnny's being haunted has skyrocketed."

"By how much?" Betty asked

"A gazillion times, if not more."

As Betty reached the door she turned and asked, "Who are the new owners?"

"Who else? Old Man Harney," the woman answered. "The richest S.O. B. in town."

FOURTEEN

A dozen people sat around a table located in a banquet room at the Happy Bison Café, located two blocks off of Main Street. The monthly meeting of Ghosts Hunters United was about to begin.

Seated next to Evan, Tillie asked, "Wow, there's lot of members here. No little league game tonight?"

Before Evan could respond, a gray haired woman across from them whispered, "Rained out."

At the head of the table Sarge said, "As most of you know, we have two guests tonight. One is Tillie McFinn from the Chicago chapter of Ghost Hunters United."

The entire group shifted toward her and said in unison, "Hi, Tillie."

Tillie forced herself not to respond, "Hi. I'm Tillie McFinn and I'm addicted to ghosts."

Instead, she gave a slight wave of her hand.

Sarge continued, "Seated next to her is Evan who will be doing an article for the Dakota Daily. "

Oohs and ahhs drifted across the room.

Sarge added, "Hopefully by the time the article is written, we'll have convinced Evan that ghosts are real."

A barrage of phrases tossed at Evan included comments such as "Come over to my house if you don't believe" to "I've seen twenty myself."

119

Sarge tapped the table with a small gavel. "Now to the order of business. First of all, if you haven't paid your ten-dollar yearly dues yet, please do so at the end. Second, have there been any sightings this week? Any missing objects? Any voices coming through a television that is turned off?"

An elderly woman seated next to Sarge raised her hand.

Sarge said, "Yes, Lorraine?"

She answered, "I think I saw something outside of my window a few nights ago."

"Can you describe it?" Sarge asked.

She answered, "No, I just thought I saw something. I didn't actually see it."

Tillie refused to acknowledge Evan's look of disbelief he shot her way.

Lorraine continued, "Oh! And my toaster oven started sounding funny, like it was gurgling as it toasted my buns."

Evan placed his hand over his mouth to stop from laughing. Tillie covered hers, as well.

Sarge nodded as he wrote the member's comments on a notepad.

Lorraine added, "And there's one more thing, my knitting bag's missing."

That peaked Tillie's interest.

Tillie asked, "Did the bag happen to be empty, Lorraine?"

Lorraine said, "There was a small skein of yarn inside it, but nothing else."

Tillie inquired, "Did you make a police report?"

A member to Tillie's left answered, "Why should she? Buckley never believes any of us. He thinks we're all suffering from dementia. Even the young ones."

Sarge asked, "Lorraine, were any of your windows opened?"

"No," she answered.

120

"Do you happen to know if your door was locked?" Sarge looked toward Evan and said, "I'm not prying. Whenever we investigate any paranormal activity, we insist on ruling out any non-supernatural connection. And if her doors were unlocked…"

Evan nodded in understanding.

Sarge continued, "As far as you know Lorraine, there is no way a burglar could gain entry into your house?"

Lorraine answered, "Not unless he's a leprechaun…"

Tillie's eyebrows rose in anticipation.

Lorraine continued, "—and can fit through a doggie door."

Tillie's eyebrows lowered to normal.

Sarge asked, "How long has your bag been missing?"

"Three days."

As Sarge wrote down Lorraine's final response, he read out loud, "Lorraine's knitting bag mysteriously disappeared, starting Tuesday." He set down his pen. "Are there any other comments, sightings, or questions before we begin tonight's presentation?" Sarge paused for a response, and then added, "Alrighty then, let's take a five-minute coffee break before we start our slide show, Undead in Deadwood."

The members stood up and headed toward the back of the room and gathered around a silver urn. Tillie and Evan remained seated. She asked, "Is the group planning on going with us to Harney's after the meeting?"

Evan answered, "There's been a change of plans. Harney told Sarge we can't come back. Sarge thinks the guy's freaked out by us finding the nugget."

Tillie responded, "I think he'd be happy. He's thirty-six hundred dollars richer."

121

Evan shrugged, "From what I hear, money has never brought Harney a moment of happiness."

"Really?"

"As soon as he gets one dollar, he regrets it isn't two. The rumor is that he has every dime he's ever earned."

"So, he's not some poor merchant?"

Evan gave a disgruntled chuckle. "His family's one of the oldest and richest in the Dakotas. The first Harney arrived during the gold rush. Supposedly, Old Man Harney is the great grandson of one of the original upstairs girls."

"Wow!" Tillie responded, not in shock at Harney's lineage, but the possibilities that came with it. She said, "If that's true, then maybe the spirit in the basement, the one I immediately detected as an upstairs girl was really..."

"The old man's great grandmother," Evan said, and for the first time looked as if he might be starting to believe in spirits.

Tillie asked, "And if that's the case, how is the kid ghost in the attic connected? The one who left their handprints on the window."

"Well, since we're banned from Harney's, I guess we'll never know," Evan answered.

Tillie responded bluntly, "There's no way I'm leaving this town until I do know. No way. Even if I..." Tillie stopped talking.

One thing she knew for sure in this life was to never tell the press you might be willing to commit a crime. Especially when you already knew you were planning to do it.

∞

122

Twenty minutes before closing, Codey strolled into Harney's Jewelry. His mother's insistence that he give her 'some space' had him walking up and down Main Street. Of course, he could have tailed his mom without her knowing it. But, she'd crucify him if she found out. Codey wasn't afraid of too many things in his life except grizzlies, gun-waving drunks, and his mother's disapproval. Her look of "What did you do?" still gave him the same heebeegeebees he felt at eleven years old.

Though Deadwood was a lively gambling town, the history of the area interested him more. Besides, he wasn't much of a gambler, drinker or a risk taker. It was people who intrigued him. As a kid he avoided riding the roller coaster. The only wagering he participated in normally was the occasional lottery pool at work. Even then, he'd only do it when the stakes were five hundred million dollars or more.

He'd make the same joke every time he threw in his dollar, "Winning anything less wouldn't be worth the effort to drive to the lottery office to claim it."

Codey wasn't interested in getting "hammered", a favorite vacation activity of many of his cohorts. His alcohol limit was two beers, max. If he had more he didn't turn reckless or act out of control. Nor did he continue to drink until he passed out. He simply fell asleep. His genetic makeup, intolerance for risk taking and inability to overly imbibe had him stuck at being the perpetual good guy.

Still, he stopped at a few of the gaming establishments along the way to Harney's. Codey knew the basics of three-card poker and decided to risk ten bucks at each gambling venue he passed. By the time he walked into Harney's, he was a hundred dollars ahead.

"Can I help you?" The combination of a growl and question emerged from the throat of the elderly man.

123

"Just looking," Codey responded. The man nodded before shuffling toward the back of the store.

A half a dozen customers roamed the aisles or paused in front of the glitzy display cases.

The abundance of black hills gold glistened through the glass. Solid gold nuggets and small bags of gold dust were available for purchase. Rows of bracelets, rings, earrings and pendants were displayed.

Three teenage girls clustered around the engagement ring display. Their giggling alone would drive Codey to distraction. He'd end up buying Christine the wrong ring so he could get away from the effervescent trio. Instead, he strolled over to the aisle featuring colorful dream catchers or stone carvings of bison. He'd wait for the girls to leave and if they didn't, he'd come back tomorrow.

The entry bell rang causing Codey to look up. The man entering the store was Lame Johnny's Hotel manager, Chad Harney. He stomped to the back of the store towards the frail, grumpy man.

Instinctively, Codey placed his hand on his hip, but the only thing his hand landed on was his belt. His holster and gun was where it should be, back in Chicago. Still, he didn't like the hotel manger's demeanor. True, he may well have been a disgruntled customer, but Codey's gut told him otherwise. He moved slowly down the aisle until he was within earshot of the quarrelling duo.

"I got your friggin message, Grandpa. Really? You're bringing that up again? After what? Twenty years?" The young man sputtered. "I told you then I didn't steal your frickin' nugget but you never believed me."

Ah, family dispute. Codey stepped back from the two until he could no longer hear the words exchanged. Whatever was being said was none of his business. He realized the confrontation wouldn't end soon. But the mood for buying your one true love a symbol of eternal devotion was ruined. He'd come back in the morning when the atmosphere would be more suitable, and perhaps even giggle-free.

FIFTEEN

Shoot!" Tillie said, before laughing at her reaction to a non-winning spin of two blue sevens and a single blank space. "Guess I'm becoming greedy, eh?"

"Easy to do," Betty responded, slipping in her second ten-dollar bill of the evening. The two women were seated in the penny slot area of the gaming room at Lame Johnny's. Even at eleven p.m., the establishment was bustling with gamblers, partiers, winners and losers shouting with joy or moaning with disappointment.

She'd been gambling for only a few minutes when Tillie arrived, unexpectedly. Within the first few minutes, Tillie won three hundred and sixty-six dollars on a penny slot. Betty was down another five bucks. Betty asked, "Why are you back early? It's not even the witching hour. Have you given up on finding ghosts in this town?"

"Not at all," Tillie answered, pressing the play max button. "In fact, I'm convinced one particular female presence is aching to contact me in private."

"Why?"

"I think she feels we're kindred spirits."

"How so?"

"Because I'm a former bad-girl. She probably thinks I understand her plight," Tillie answered, hitting the play button again.

126

"Former bad-girl?" Betty teased, though Tillie could hardly be considered bad. Only a hint of playful wickedness would emerge every now and then.

"Trust me, I've turned into such a goody-goody, I might as well be Amish," Tillie answered.

Betty didn't respond with a rebuttal. Not too many Amish wore Spandex, glittery tube tops and push-up bras that created mountains out of, well, mountains.

"And you're sure it's female?" Betty asked as the spinning wheels on Betty's machine resulted in another loss.

"Yep, and I'm pretty sure she's an upstairs girl."

"Really?" Betty couldn't help but become trapped in her driver's web of storytelling. A dead prostitute trying to make contact with Tillie had Betty sitting literally on the edge of her swivel seat.

"How do you know she's trying to contact you?" Betty watched the reels in front of her spin. When they stopped, only two bars, and nothing else landed directly in her view. Shoot! Betty was now at the limit of her gambling budget per day while on tour.

"At first, I only felt her presence, "Tillie explained. "You know the feeling that someone is looking over your shoulder and when you turn around, no one's there?"

Betty answered, "I get that all the time. But, that doesn't mean a ghost is…"

Tillie interrupted. "—Sure it does. Then I smelled…"

"—Lavender?" Betty asked, by now becoming familiar with the lore surrounding Tillie's avocation.

"The scent surrounded me. The real kicker was hearing the bells she wore. That proved she was a working girl."

"Bells? Why would it prove that?" Betty asked.

Tillie continued, "In medieval times in Italy, city officials forced prostitutes to wear bells on their heads, or their shawls."

"Their version of the Scarlett A?"

"Kind of," Tillie answered. "Centuries later a few madams kept up the practice, either as a joke, or as a punishment. By the way, that little tidbit of history trivia is a direct result of my incarceration."

"A jailed prostitute told you that?"

"More than one," Tillie replied.

"Where were you when you heard the bells ring?"

"Both times at Harney's. Once in the cellar and the other time in his attic."

"The ghost traveled from one floor to another?" Betty wondered why she was suddenly reacting as if the entities were real.

"They were following me," Tillie said, taking a moment to brush back her curly red hair from her forehead.

Betty asked, "Can they do that?"

Tillie answered, "They basically can do whatever they want, although they usually like to stay in one place. That takes less energy than moving about."

Betty hit play again. "You do know that many of the buildings along Main Street were brothels at one time?"

"And more than likely, so was Harney's."

"Well, that explains what the More stands for, I guess." Betty added, pushing the button before realizing the machine was out of credits. "That's that. I'm through gambling for the day."

Tillie said, "I'm way ahead. Want me to give you a few bucks?"

"Nah, have to stay within my daily limit, or I'm screwed."

"And not in the good way," Tillie added.

"And not in the good way," Betty responded and watched as Tillie pressed the payout button on her machine. A paper voucher emerged showing a three-hundred and sixty-eight-dollar credit.

"Are you going back to the room?" Betty asked, adjusting her shoulder strap bag.

Tillie answered, "Nah, there's something I want to do."

As Betty stood, Jerome Anderson walked up to her side. She said, "Good evening, Jerome. Is there something I can help you with?" Betty was used to her clients walking up to her at any time of the day and in any place. In fact, she welcomed it.

He said, "I wanted to add my name to that tour you were talking about."

She asked, "The one to the BBQ at a working ranch, or the gold mind tour?"

Jerome inquired, "Is the mine tour the one where we can pan for gold?"

"It certainly is," Betty answered. So far ten of her riders had already registered for the event.

Jerome gave a coy grin before adding, "Can you put me down for two tickets? Hannah's going with me."

"Sure will," Betty answered, not taking the chance to catch the expression on Tillie's face. If she did, there would be a good chance they'd be rolling on the floor in laughter within minutes.

Jerome strolled off in a slow but cocky strut.

As soon as he was out of hearing range Tillie asked, "Hannah and Jerome are dating?"

"I think they might be," Betty answered. "Didn't you notice that Jerome had a glint of desire in his eyes, if you know what I mean."

Tillie stood up, and answered, "I do, but you're wrong."

Betty asked, "Why.

Tillie shrugged. "Jerome's seventy-eight. If he's got a glint of anything in his eyes, it's probably a cataract."

∞

From the alleyway behind Harney's, Tillie watched as a small yellow light flickered through the smudged attic window. In her heart, she knew the upstairs girl had a message for her and her alone.

Of course, if Betty or Evan were standing next to her, they'd suggest the light wasn't coming from the attic at all. That it was the window's reflection from the street lamps. Tillie believed otherwise. Her new friend was beckoning her.

Tillie's fears of stepping inside the building grew. The fact that there had been a strong cigar odor earlier didn't help her trepidation. An evil spirit could masquerade as a good being, for a brief amount of time. But that was more than enough.

Tillie took one more look at the flickering light before heading up the steps that climbed alongside the back of the building. The stairs connected to the upper level and the hallway that housed the Harney's rental apartment. It was the same hallway that provided the pull-down set of stairs to the attic.

The front and back entrances to Harney's actual store had excellent security. The entryways were steel doors plastered with decals declaring the property was monitored by video security. But Tillie knew that off-putting decals were cheaper than purchasing an actual surveillance system. The deadbolt lock at the top of the steps was easy to pick. It was a skill Tillie learned

130

early in life when her mom kept losing their apartment keys at one Chicago bar after another.

There were no lights on in the tenants' apartment. The residents were likely asleep in their apartment. Perfect. It would allow Tillie to lower the foldable stairs and leave them that way until she climbed back down.

She slipped a miner's flashlight on her head, and pulled the rope that lowered the folding steps and climbed up. Once both of her feet were planted firmly on the attic floor, she moved her head slowly around, as her headlight canvassed the area. There was no smell of flowers to welcome her, nor did any bells ring out a hello. She couldn't feel a presence, at all.

Tillie cautiously walked over to the window. The windows appeared to have been recently cleaned. She had a feeling that if she could turn on a light switch the entire place would appear swept and spotless. Perhaps Harney had his sent his cleaning crew up, looking for more gold.

It was then Tillie heard the sounds that scared her more than any spirit she'd ever encountered.

A slurred male voice traveled down the hallway below. "Who left the stairs down?"

The apartment residents weren't sleeping after all. They'd been out drinking and were returning home, smashed. Fortunately, they were drunk enough not to notice the exterior door's lock picked open.

An equally slurred female response mumbled back, "Probably the cleaners. They were in the attic earlier? Remember?"

"Oh yeah," He answered and followed his words with a loud burp.

"You gonna check it out?" the woman asked.

"I guess," he responded.

Harney's tenant climbed up the unfolded staircase. The only miracle Tillie could hope for was that he

131

didn't have a flashlight on him. Tillie clicked off her miner's forehead light and cautiously curled up on the floor, directly behind a few boxes. If the light coming off Main Street didn't illuminate her, she might get away with her trespassing.

From below the woman asked, "See anything?"

The man poked his head through the opening and yelled, "Anybody up here?"

He waited for a few seconds before declaring, "It's empty." He headed back down the steps and within a few seconds folded the stairs up and lifted them to the ceiling, closing off the attic's entrance.

Tillie would have to wait it out. She couldn't dare to move an inch for at least a few hours. By that time the tenants should be sound asleep. Then she'd creep over to the stairs and figure out a way of lowering them, unfolding the contraption in the process. Until then there was nothing to do but wait and see if Bella would show up and wish her a good night.

∞

"Mrs. Chance," a stern voice boomed from behind and echoed off the walnut walls of the lobby.

Betty turned, a defensive smile plastered across her face. Whoever reached out to her at such a late hour in the evening didn't sound like a happy camper.

"Chad," she said pleasantly, hoping a welcoming tone would change his surly disposition. Whatever was upsetting the manager wasn't good.

Chad hustled up to her and stopped abruptly. He crossed his arms in front of his chest and said, "I was wondering if you would do me a favor?"

From his demeanor, Betty already knew the favor was a demand.

"Of course," she answered politely.

Chad instructed, "From this moment on, please do not harass our employees."

"Harass? I've never…"

He interrupted, "—Or offer them bribes to gossip about our internal affairs."

Uh, oh! Somehow Chad knew about the discussion she and the maid had earlier in the day.

Betty responded, "I didn't give a bribe your employee. I tipped her because she was kind enough to let me check out the suite. I merely wanted to see if our clients would…"

He interrupted again, "—I believe you already know what the suites look like. As a travel host. I'm sure you've read in our brochures all the suites are identical. Besides, didn't you and your son already barge into one of our suites to check out the whirlpool incident?"

Betty said, "We didn't barge into anything. My son is a Chicago…"

Chad interrupted again. "—I know who your son is, Mrs. Chance. I also know that your tour driver is an ex-con."

That surprised Betty. How could Chad have inside knowledge like that, unless he had a connection to law enforcement? And why in the heck was he checking out her employees in the first place?

"Actually Tillie's life, current or past, is none of your business," Betty informed him.

"Actually," Chad responded back sarcastically, "it is. Anything that puts this hotel in danger is my business."

"Danger? What are you talking about?" and then it hit her. The what Chad was referring to was Johnson's murder. "Are you saying that because Tillie was once imprisoned, that somehow she is connected to…"

133

He held his palm up to stop her. "All I am saying is that I have my eye on you. You should know once you and your tour check out of the hotel, you, your son, and Tillie are never welcome here again. Take A Chance Tours is banned from Lame Johnny's."

Chad turned and stomped his way back to the front desk. The term flabbergasted came to Betty's mind in describing how she felt. Whatever was going on with Chad Harney was intimidating. There was no reason for him to have such a reaction to Sasha inferring ghosts were invented to stir up business. The hotel management had to assume that most tour operators and guests would probably think the same, even without asking.

There was also no reason for his extreme level of anger. Not unless Chad was hiding something, something he was afraid Betty's poking around might discover. That, Betty decided, was silly of him to have worried about. Before he accosted her, Betty had no legitimate reason to investigate anything about the hotel management, not a single one.

But now, after listening to Chad's rant, she did.

SIXTEEN

Tillie's eyelashes flittered as the sun warmed her face. She adjusted her body and cradled her head in her arms to avoid the light coming in from the window. Her body retreated into a fetal position.

Damn hotel air conditioning, Tillie mumbled, reaching down to pull the covers up over her…wait a minute… Dammit! She swore out loud and then covered her mouth in fear. The last thing she needed was for anyone to hear her. Instead of leaving Harney's attic in the wee hours of the morning like she'd planned, she'd fallen asleep.

She pulled her body up, and stared out the grimy windows toward Main Street. At eight a.m. tourists were strolling along the sidewalks, Styrofoam coffee cups in hand. Store employees were unlocking doors. Gamblers' outlines shown through casino windows. Deadwood was fully awake while she was groggy from a fitful night's sleep and wondering if she'd be arrested within a matter of minutes.

She'd vowed to never, ever do anything illegal again. While driving, Tillie stayed within the posted speed limits. She paid her taxes early and was too fearful to take exemptions even if she deserved them. If she noticed a dollar lying on the floor of a store she'd hand it over to Lost and Found.

Tillie wanted nothing to threaten her freedom. Spending a decade of your life in prison could do that

135

to a person; though there were many convicts who did the opposite. As soon as they were released, they started committing crimes as if they wanted to be tossed back into the security of three hots and a cot.

Now, she wondered if she wasn't the same. Could the lure of seeing Bella really be so strong, she'd risk losing her freedom? What was it about Bella that clutched at her heart so much Tillie's common sense was blocked?

Okay, enough with beating herself up she decided. There'd be enough time for that later, especially if she was tossed in the slammer. But for now, she needed to escape without being noticed by the tenants, or Harney.

Tillie tiptoed around the attic floor, each creek of the floorboard causing her heart to jump. Before she lost consciousness to sleep she'd figured out how to lower the retracting stairs. All she needed was a stick or a pole. In the corner she discovered an old straw broom leaning against the wall.

Edging over the opening, Tillie placed her ear against it. As far as she could tell, there were no sounds. It was still early and the tenants had been on a bender, they were probably sound asleep. She pushed the access door with the broom, causing it to lower halfway, but half of the steps were still folded upwards. Using the broomstick again, she caught the edge of a step and pushed it, causing the folded steps to not only open outward, but to clunk loudly on the hallway floor with a thump.

She waited to see if the tenants ran out of their apartment to check what was going on. Breathing a sigh of relief, she gingerly headed down the steps, one creak at a time. As soon as she stepped off the bottom rung, she lifted the apparatus into the ceiling. Tillie rushed toward the exit door to the outside steps. She was within ten feet of escape when she heard two men arguing.

136

The man's voice shouted, "I'm telling you for the second time in two days, it wasn't me. Stop leaving accusatory messages on my answering machine. You're upsetting my wife."

"Then who was it?" came the grizzled reply from what had to be a senior citizen. In a mocking tone he asked, "Do you want me to believe it was Bella?"

"Yeah, that's right, Bella," the young man shot back. "Great-great grannie's frickin' ghost."

"Next time I'm calling the cops," the old guy said before hacking up a mountain goat.

"You do that," the younger man replied bitterly. "Because what am I going to lose? My inheritance?"

A door slammed shut. She waited a few minutes before exiting, in case whoever was angry lingered in the back alley. She counted down from two hundred and when she hit zero, opened the door to the outside and fled down the stairs.

As soon as she reached the alley, she whispered Thank God. As far as she could see there was no one else around her. She turned left and began running toward the street when she heard his voice.

"Tillie?" the voice questioned.

She swirled around and standing ten feet behind her was the sheriff.

"Out for your morning jog?" Buckley asked.

Tillie didn't know if he'd caught a glimpse of her leaving the upper level of Harney's, or not. Smiling back at him she said, "Nah, I was … well," she paused, not knowing what to say next.

"I know what you're up to," the sheriff insisted.

Tillie asked weakly, "You do?"

"Sure, you're ghost hunting. Your outfit's a dead giveaway, no pun intended," he said and added a coy smile. "Your outfit's from the movie Ghostbusters, right?"

Tillie nodded.

Buckley asked, "Are you ready for our breakfast date? Or is it too early? I can wait."

"Now is okay, if you don't mind the outfit."

"Are you kidding," Buckley said, his eyes scanning every inch of her. "I love it."

∞

The best way Betty knew how to begin an investigation was by first going for a stroll. She referred to it as her walking meditation, though she wasn't sure if there were any Buddhist monks who listened to soundtracks on their iPod as they stepped through life. But for Betty, listening to a film score, while walking aimlessly yet open to possibilities, shifted her mind into a problem-solving machine.

Outdoors, the temperature was in the low 60s. Perfect for walking the streets and alleys of Deadwood. Though she was still on the clock, there was no reason not to roam. She was only a text or cell phone call away from her clients.

As soon as she exited the hotel, Betty slipped her earbuds in and hit play. The award winning 1962 soundtrack, How The West Was Won began. The musical score was another example of how a movie could be not great, but the soundtrack to it, spectacular. One of the things she loved about soundtracks was how heroic they often made her feel. She felt like a heroine as the first dynamic notes assaulted her ears.

Betty glanced at her watch. It was a little after nine a.m. and she'd yet to see Tillie or her son that morning. More than likely, they were still in their beds. When the two women parted ways last evening, her driver claimed she had something she wanted to do. Betty understood the something meant Tillie was going on the prowl alone, looking for ghouls, or whatever.

Betty reset her pedometer to zero earlier. Over two thousand steps were already registered. With any luck she'd make it to ten thousand by noon. She moved down the sidewalk at a brisk pace, passing by merchants and casinos. Even the glitter of Black Hills Gold in Harney's didn't tempt her. As usual, she was wise enough to leave any cash and credit cards in the wall safe back in her room. If she couldn't pay for it, she couldn't buy it.

Betty was a strong-willed woman, but not strong enough to walk past The Squealing Squirrel without heading in for "just a little treat". Giving in to that sort of temptation could easily turn into a bacchanalian chocolate orgy. As soon as she neared the Squirrel she increased her speed and passed it quickly, refusing to either inhale or look at the window display. Within a few seconds she reached a corner and allowed herself to breathe again. She made an immediate turn to the left and headed into the residential area, where there would be fewer culinary enticements.

The narrow streets were filled with small clapboard houses and larger Victorian homes, some converted into weekly vacation rentals or B&Bs. The structures butted against the slopes of the Black Hills. Because it was a Saturday, a few yard sales were in progress or residents were mowing yards or weeding their property.

Betty saw her standing in the middle of a fenced yard, beer can in hand, while a puppy raced in circles around the woman's feet. Two grown German Shepherds were chained up in the yard, barking furiously, their water and food bowls empty. She was the hotel maid that Betty tipped the day before in exchange for information on ghosts at Lame Johnny's.

Betty walked up to the picket fence gate and said, "Excuse me."

The barking increased and Betty prayed the chains didn't break. If they did, each of the German Shepherds could easily jump over the gate and attack. Betty wasn't normally afraid of dogs, but the viciousness they displayed had her on high alert. The one thing you did not mess with in this life was an angry guard dog.

The woman took a sip of her Coors light as the barking became louder and more ferocious. She yelled, "Shut up you mutts." The dogs immediately became quiet and cowered in fear. "You'd think as much time as my husband spends training them, they'd know to shut up on their own."

Betty asked, "Do you remember me from yesterday at the hotel?"

"Sure do," the woman said. "You want your ten bucks back?"

"No, of course not, I was wondering if..." Betty halted and then blurted out her fear. "Did my asking you about Lame Johnny's get you fired?"

Losing a job in a town as small as Deadwood could have dire consequences. Employment opportunities were often few and far between. Perhaps that was why she was drinking so early in the morning.

The woman laughed loudly before saying, "Heavens, no. I wish he had. It would take a lot more than that to get my husband to fire me."

"Your husband?"

"Yeah, Chad Harney. He manages the hotel, as well as doing a ton of other jobs that need doing. Our employees don't seem to last too long."

Relieved, Betty said, "I'm so happy to hear you're..."

The woman interrupted. "—Chad told me he banned you. Sorry about that. You didn't do anything

140

wrong. Sometimes Chad's temper gets the best of him."

Betty nodded.

The woman took another long sip before adding, "He'll forget about it a month or so, once he realizes the money it'll cost the old man."

Betty said, "A tour company is good for business."

Mrs. Harney responded, "Tell you the truth, Chad's never been good with money, keeping it or making it. When I married into the family, I thought I was set for life..." Chad's wife looked around at the patched yard and rundown house. "What do they say, be careful what you wish for? I always wanted to be a Harney, and now I am."

Betty smiled slightly in return, not knowing quite what to say. She wondered if the woman's early morning drinking habits impeded her judgment about talking to a stranger about her personal life. She said, "I'm sorry."

The woman released an ironic laugh and said, "Ah, don't bother to feel sad for me. I was only bitching. Chad's okay, and better than anyone else in his family, that's for sure."

Betty asked, "Is the Harney family big?"

"Not anymore," the woman answered. "Just the old man and my husband. Chad's dad died years ago, right after his mom ran off. Chad's been kissing the old man's butt ever since."

"Well, there's you, too. You're family." Betty smiled.

She smirked. "Not really. The Harney clan doesn't think any one is related unless they're blood. As far as the old man is concerned, I'm not even a member of the family." She used her strength to crush the empty beer can in her hand. She tossed it perfectly into the waste can, ten feet away. As soon as it landed, she pulled out a cigarette and lit it.

141

Either the woman had no boundaries when it came to sharing family problems with strangers, or she was at the end of her rope. One thing Betty had noticed throughout the years, when people were at their breaking point, they'd share that fact with anyone.

Betty said, "I'm glad to hear you didn't lose your job. I worried about that. Have a good day." As Betty turned to leave one of the puppies was trying to poke his head though a small opening in the picket fence.

Mrs. Harney yelled, "Bella, stop that."

Betty stopped walking and swirled around, asking, "You named your puppy Bella?"

Picking up the pup, the woman answered, "My husband did. Chad always has to have one of his dogs named that. As soon as one Bella goes missing, another one takes their place."

Betty asked, "Do you lose a lot of dogs?"

Suddenly the woman's demeanor changed. She was no longer an overfriendly, beer-guzzling chatterbox. Her face became hardened. "Sorry, I have work to do," she said and rushed back inside the house, bringing the yelping puppy with her.

Betty hurried down the street, hoping her swift exit and disappearance would help settle the barking dogs down. It wasn't until the next block that the meditative effects of her soundtrack kicked in again, and her thinking became clear and focused.

Wyoming had mentioned a "friend" who worked at the hotel and that she wasn't staying at their place because they had these "nasty dogs". If the friend was Wyoming's pimp like Betty deduced, then her pimp was none other than Chad Harney.

SEVENTEEN

More coffee, Sheriff?" The plumpish waitress asked in a tone so alluring it suggested The Morning Special was immediate access to her bedroom.

"Nah, I think my friend here wants to leave me A.S.A.P," Buckley shot a wink across the table at Tillie.

"Well, then she doesn't know you very well, does she?" The server said and left without offering Tillie a drop of java.

Tillie said, "I'm sorry, I don't mean to be rude. Breakfast was great, but it's been a long night and…"

Buckley interrupted, "Night? The day's just started."

Oops. Stupid comment on her part. She'd let the Sheriff believe she was out for a morning jog and not doing the walk of shame from being accidently locked in Harney's attic. She'd already spent more time with the law officer then planned. Surprisingly, her breakfast date wasn't bad. Buckley turned out to be charming. If she didn't already have a dozen men in her life chasing her, as well as a few ghosts, she might be interested.

She pulled the tab on her zipper down a few clicks, allowing a tad more cleavage to emerge. It was her own personal trick at making a man forget what she said a few seconds earlier. As soon as she saw the sheriff's eyes widen, she knew it worked. To lead him off track even more she said, "Well, I could stay for a few more minutes."

The sheriff lifted his eyes from looking directly at her chest, met her gaze and said, "That would be great."

Tillie added, "But, I'm assuming you have to get to work at some point."

The sheriff gave her a cockeyed grin. "Not really. There's not a lot of crime in Deadwood. Petty stuff mostly, checks bouncing, robbery, a few kids pulling pranks…" He stopped in midstream as his face took on a sullen expression. "That is, until two days ago."

The sheriff glanced at his watch as if he suddenly remembered there were more important things to do than to flirt with a vivacious bus driver—like finding a killer at large in his hometown.

But now Tillie had changed her mind, and wanted to carry on the conversation about the homicide. Whatever information she could find out, she'd share with Betty. If she knew her friend at all, by now Betty was in full amateur sleuth mode.

Tillie said, "I know I shouldn't ask, but are you close to finding the guy who did it?"

The sheriff gulped his last bit of coffee down. "I can't really talk about that."

"I understand. I was only wondering if I should be worried about walking the streets alone at night."

The sheriff said, "You don't have to worry. One thing I can share is the killing wasn't random."

Tillie understood immediately what the sheriff was implying. The murderer knew the victim. It wasn't stranger danger, after all. In fact, it was like most homicides—the culprit was either a family member or a friend.

∞

Betty stopped dead in her tracks. A half a block in front of her the sheriff and Tillie dressed in her ghosting ensemble, walked out of a coffee shop. Betty managed to catch Tillie's eye who then responded by giving Betty a hand gesture that indicated for her to wait.

Betty watched as her friend shook Buckley's hand goodbye, laughing while she refused his attempt to kiss her on the cheek. She also noticed the Sheriff ogling Tillie's ample rear. As soon as Tillie reached Betty, the Sheriff walked away in the opposite direction.

Betty asked, "Is the Sheriff a member of G.H.U.?"

Tillie shook her head. "Nah, he ran in to me when I was heading back to the hotel this morning. He insisted I have breakfast with him."

"What do you mean 'back to the hotel'? Have you been up all night on a search?"

Tillie answered sheepishly, "Nah, I kind of fell asleep on location. I didn't wake up until the morning sun hit my face."

Betty asked, "Where were you?" Wherever the location was, it may not have been safe for a woman alone. Knowing Tillie's devotion to her passion, she could have fallen asleep on top of Calamity Jane's grave.

"That's not important," Tillie answered.

By Tillie's abrupt response, Betty realized that wherever Tillie was, she probably shouldn't have been there in the first place. Betty didn't push for an answer. Though they were close friends, her driver's off-hour activities were none of her business.

The women continued their walk down the sidewalk, past shops, casinos and outdoor vendors. Betty said, "So, tell me about the breakfast."

Tillie teased, "I had eggs over easy, hash browns, sausage patties..."

Betty interrupted, "—You know what I'm asking. What's the Sheriff like?"

Tillie admitted, "Like most good looking hunks. He's cocky, sure of himself, and sexy as hell."

"Did he tell you he was divorced?"

"He did. He said his daughter's running all over town, posting flyers of some lost dog she found. She ran into Codey."

"Really?" Betty said. That surprised her. Her son wasn't the type to go around introducing himself to women. The woman must have approached him first.

"His daughter was posting signs about some lost dog when they met. She told the sheriff that Codey fell head over heels in love with the dog at first sight."

"That's not surprising. He always does that," Betty answered. If it were possible, Codey loved animals more than she did.

The women stopped to check out a line of western clothing in a store window. Tillie pointed at a pair of leather chaps and teased, "Are you wondering if those assless pants come in plus sizes?"

Betty responded, "If they do, then I will have to buy them three sizes smaller than I normally do." The duo started walking again. Betty asked, "Did the sheriff mention anything about the murder?"

"Only that he's convinced it wasn't a random killing."

"That's good to know," Bettys responded. If there was a reason for the murder, then it made it less terrifying. It wasn't some psycho deciding to kill for the heck of it.

"Good morning Betty," two of her passengers said at exactly the same time as they passed by her.

"Good morning," Betty answered back. "Have fun today."

"We will," they said, and shuffled down the streets, their arms filled with bags full of merchandise.

Main Street was packed with many of Betty's clients. She encountered three more before arriving at Lame Johnny's entrance. In front of the valet service, she watched a dozen of her riders stepping into the shuttle that would escort them to the gold mine tour. The last two to board the bus were Jerome and Hannah.

Tillie said, "Would you look at that? Jerome offered Hannah his hand to help her up the steps and…"

Betty interrupted, "she actually took it. Looks like the Dragon Lady of Calumet has put Mr. Anderson under a spell."

"Yep, as soon as she kisses him, Jerome will turn into a frog."

EIGHTEEN

I can't believe you eat like that and don't weigh six hundred pounds," Codey said, sitting down across from his mother.

Betty asked her son to meet her at the buffet at one. She arrived at noon. The three plates in front of her held half-eaten samples of the dishes offered at Blackie's. Betty wasn't being gluttonous or wasteful. She was in the midst of writing her food review.

Pushing aside her notebook Betty said, "If I ate like this every day, I would weight that, if not more."

"So would I," her son answered. "But, you're doing really good at keeping your weight off. I'm proud of you."

Since her divorce three years ago, Codey became her cheerleader of a son when it came to getting fit. He even bought her a pedometer. He cheered when she lost weight, and hugged her when she stayed the same. If she gained a pound or two back, he hugged her even harder and told her not to worry.

Betty replied, "You might want to try their rotisserie grilled steak? It's the lunch special today."

"That sounds great," Codey said standing up to head to the live action cooking station. "Anything else I should know about?"

"The chocolate is fountain running at full speed."

Codey interrupted. "—Again, why is it that you don't weigh six hundred pounds? I can't believe what you chose to do for a living. It's like you face the temptations of being on a vacation twenty-four seven, every single day."

Betty laughed. "I do. And know what? That is exactly what I love about being a tour host."

The minute Codey headed toward the grill station, Betty focused on her final notations. If she was lucky, she'd finish the review and post it on her blog before leaving Deadwood tomorrow afternoon.

"An assortment of side dishes showcasing produce from local farms are featured. My favorites were the creamy Potato gratin, baked fingerling jacket potatoes rolled in sea salt and herbs, sautéed spinach, curry-roasted cauliflower, roasted sweet pepper risotto, and carrots glazed with South Dakota honey. The butternut squash was smothered in maple syrup infused with a citrusy taste. A slice of the cinnamon spiced Rotisserie Chicken made my tongue do the happy dance. My Rib Eye was charred on the outside and a uniform medium rare on the inside. The juices poured out of it when I cut into it. The only way I can describe the meat is by calling it meltingly tender. Blackie's Monkey Bread, was well, meh. But the Carrot cake had the perfect amount of sweetness with a delectable cream cheese frosting, accented with what else? Roasted sunflower seeds."

Codey made his way back to the table, balancing two plates toppling with food. He slid into his chair mumbling, "Good thing I did five miles this morning."

"Speaking of that, Tillie told me you met the sheriff's daughter yesterday when you were out on a run?"

"I did. Well, I actually met her dog first ... I mean the lost dog. Buckley's kid found a chocolate Labrador a few miles outside of town. There weren't any tags, so she assumed the dog was lost, or abandoned." Codey ingested a forkful of mountain trout and rolled his eyes upwards as if to give thanks to heaven.

149

Betty commented, "Who in their right mind would toss away a Lab?"

Codey answered, "I totally agree. You do know that is my favorite breed of dog?"

"Yes, along with every other breed."

"Well, that's true. It's kind of ironic I am a dog lover…"

Betty grinned. "Because you are also such a devoted cat owner?"

Codey nodded as he cut into his charred steak. Fortunately, Codey's fiancée was just as enamored with furry companions. If their best friends were to be members of their wedding party, they'd all be the four-legged kind.

"Have you looked at any engagement rings in town?"

Codey said, "I was going to but a gaggle of teenage girls kept me from getting anywhere near the display."

"Were you at Harney's?"

"Yep," Codey responded while smearing sweet butter over his steaming baked potato.

"The hotel manager, Chad Harney is his grandson."

"Yeah, I figured that out," Codey answered. "Chad stormed into the store when I was there, upset about something that happened twenty years ago. Or upset that his grandfather was still upset about it is more like it."

"I can see that happening," Betty responded before taking a sip from her cup of coffee.

Codey gave her a confused look. "Why?" he asked.

"Chad's wife told me he has a temper. Sounds like the whole family does."

Codey stopped eating. "So tell me, how quickly do you learn about everything that is going on in a town? Is it a few minutes after arrival? A few hours?"

Betty was only half-kidding when she said, "Not that quickly. It usually takes me a day or two for the basics."

"And exactly how did you meet Chad's wife?" Codey asked.

Betty could tell he wasn't amused. "Sasha's a maid here, though frankly I wonder why she's not earning her living as a super model. She certainly has the looks for it."

Codey asked, "Was the Harney name featured on her nametag?"

Betty shook her head. "No, she told me who she was when I stood outside her house."

"Mom!" he said in a voice loud enough to be heard two tables over.

"There's a simple explanation. I wasn't prying. I was out trying to do my daily ten thousand when I saw her drinking a can of beer in her front yard."

"What time was this?"

"Eight a.m. or so."

"Well, this keeps getting better. So you just stopped by to say hi?"

Betty admitted, "Not exactly. I was afraid I might have gotten her fired."

Codey didn't bother to say Mom one more time. He merely folded his arms and waited.

Betty continued, "Yesterday, I tipped her to answer some questions about the hotel being haunted. Her husband found out and decided I was bribing her for inside information. The next thing I knew—you, me and Tillie are banned from staying here ever again."

"Me? He banned me?" Codey asked incredulously.

"And Take A Chance Tours."

Codey unfolded his arms and began eating again. After five bites of comfort food he said, "I thought this was going to be a pleasant lunch with my mom. It's turned into one of your sitcoms. I feel like I'm Ricky

151

Ricardo screaming out Mom every few minutes instead of yelling out Lucy."

Before Codey could continue his lecture series entitled "Mom, Learn to Mind Your Business 101" Betty's client Ester walked up to their table.

Relieved to see a nonjudgmental and familiar face, Betty gushed, "Good afternoon, Ester. Are you still ahead?"

Ester responded, "Oh sure, I always am. Lady Luck seems to be my ... let's see what do my grandkids say? Oh, I remember. Lady luck is my BFF, best friend forever."

"Do you want to join my son and me?"

"No, I wanted to tell you something. I figured you'd want to know ... and ... well frankly, it's too juicy not to share."

That surprised Betty. She always assumed Hannah was the first one to spread gossip. Betty asked, "What is it?"

"You know how things have been reported as missing? Like Chuck's wallet or Hannah's troll doll?"

Betty's throat tightened. "You think something was taken from your room?

"One of my house slippers. I'm sure I had two of them when I arrived."

"Well, yeah, probably," Betty concurred.

Ester added, "I looked under the bed for it, but I couldn't see anything. Then, I checked the bathroom next, it wasn't there."

Betty asked, "Did you let security know?"

"Heavens no," Ester answered. "The slipper isn't worth anything. Besides, what is security going to do? Chase down the ghost dog and recover it for me?"

"A what?" Codey questioned.

Ester answered, "I saw the ghost dog the first night we stayed in the hotel. I went out of my room around midnight to refill my ice bucket. And there it was, standing perfectly still at the end of the hallway."

Codey asked, "How do you know it wasn't a living dog?"

Ester answered, "Because the next morning, I asked the man at the front desk if they allowed pets. I told him if they did I'd bring Bitsy with me on my next visit."

Betty inquired, "What did he say?"

"He told me they didn't and when I mentioned what I saw, he told me the hotel's secret."

Betty asked, "What?"

Ester answered, "That the ghost that's haunting this hotel is actually a dog! Makes total sense to me. I'm a cat person myself. They'd never do such a thing."

Ester walked away, as Betty and Codey sat there slightly dumbfounded by the woman's comments.

It took a few seconds before Betty mumbled, "Wow."

"Double wow," Codey responded.

Betty admitted, "Sasha did say that since the new owners of the hotel have taken over, rumors of ghosts have skyrocketed. She implied the tales were spread on purpose."

"I figured as much," her son answered.

Betty continued, "The only thing that's better than owning a casino hotel, is owning a haunted one."

"I bet."

"She also said the new owner was the same man that owns Harney's & More."

"Chad's grandfather, in other words," Codey stated.

"And no one seems to like each other very much in that family," Betty said. She hesitated for a moment, not sure if she should share the next tidbit of information with her son. She had no idea how he

153

would react or what he would do with the information. But, she decided to go for it. Her conscience wouldn't let her do otherwise. She said, "There is something that made me feel uncomfortable when I was standing outside of Chad and Sasha's house."

"What?" Codey asked, his voice immediately taking on the tone of supreme protector.

"Chad and Sasha have two German Shepherds who became very agitated when I walked up to the fence."

"That's normal. They're natural guard dogs," Codey responded.

"That isn't what bothered me. When Sasha yelled at them, they cowered in fear."

"That's not good," Codey said, his face reflecting his budding concern.

"No, they wouldn't retreat like that unless…"

"They're abused."

"There is one more thing … and I hate to use this term, but they did seem like they were..." Betty paused.

"What?" Codey demanded.

"Nasty dogs is the phrase Wyoming used when explaining why she couldn't stay at her friend's place, the friend who gave her an employee discount on her hotel room. And by friend, I think she means her…" Betty paused, waiting for Codey to finish her sentence.

"Pimp," Codey said, his expression turning into enlightenment.

Betty added in whisper, "I'm starting to think Wyoming's 'friend' could be none other than Chad Harney."

Codey responded, "I'm going to have to let the sheriff know what you just told me. It's my duty as a police officer."

Betty said, "Does that mean you're no longer on vacation?"

Codey answered, "Mom, traveling with you and Tillie, kind of means I never was."

NINETEEN

Calamity's Book Shoppe and Tea Parlor was a world apart from dinging slots or crawling around in the dark looking for traces of the undead. Located at the far edge of the town, it took a good twenty-minute walk to reach the converted Victorian House.

Tillie climbed the porch steps and entered the store. Old wooden floors creaked with her every step. The entire first floor was filled with books like her apartment back home. On the left mismatched tables covered with lace tablecloths filled the dining area. Colorful wooden chairs painted in a variety of pastels appeared sturdy and inviting. Display shelves held huge glass jars filled with loose teas, allowing customers to make their own blends. The blackboard wall menu listed scones served with Devon cream, lemon curd, an assortment of petite desserts and crustless cucumber tea sandwiches. The rest of the space was crammed with rows of bookshelves, their height reaching to the ceiling. Situated around the room were overstuffed chairs and end tables with brass reading lamps. A small calico cat meandered through the aisle until it jumped into the welcoming lap of a customer sitting in an overstuffed armchair.

A white-haired salesclerk, whose stature resembled a stacked Russian matryoshka doll, approached Tillie. She asked, "Can I help you?"

Tillie responded, "What time do you close?" She'd only planned on being at the shop for a few minutes, but now that she saw it she realized the owners would have to kick her out at closing time. Tillie treated bookstores like they were a public library. But, because she eventually left with a big bag of books, they didn't seem to mind.

"Six," the jovial woman answered. "You have a few hours to look around."

Obviously, the woman sized up Tillie correctly—a book loving nerd at heart and not a redheaded Dolly Parton impersonator others mistook her for.

"Don't forget to sample our teas," the woman replied as she shuffled off, her arms loaded with books to restock on the shelves.

"I won't," Tillie responded, knowing at some point she'd purchase the sampler tray of miniscule deserts and a teapot of Spiced Chai. At eight p.m. she was scheduled to meet Evan and Sarge for their final night together. Evan claimed he needed to do a final Q&A interview. She guessed it was to ask if she still believed in ghosts after spending three days in Deadwood. And she would ask him why he still didn't. After that, their mutual flirting would begin in earnest. It was her last night of ghosting. Perhaps it was time to allow a suggested fling to turn in to a real one.

Three bookstore patrons were sitting at the tables, their laptops open and accessing the free Wi-Fi Calamity's offered. Wisely, the owners posted a sign claiming the store was a "cell phone free" zone. The atmosphere had the same hush of reverence often encountered in a library. Tillie reached into her purse and turned the ringer off. If anyone wanted to reach her they'd have to text her.

The stacks of books were not only the latest best sellers, but a variety of pristine copies of nearly every title an author published. The store's inventory

156

consisting of ten thousand books were separated into sections. Mystery and romance books seemed to be largest. But instead of searching out the latest mystery by Betty Webb or Kaye George, Tillie headed to the Regional section.

Her fingers brushed across the spines of the books in front of her. The topics ran the gamut from the history of South Dakota, to the spirit and grit of the pioneers, the Wounded Knee Massacre and finally gut-wrenching encounters with those who survived a grizzly bear attack. Dozens of coffee-table books were devoted to the Badlands, alone. Others captured the images of the Black Hills, Mount Rushmore, or the wildlife in the area, with bison being the most popular.

Two specific books caught her eye and she pulled them off the shelf. Then, for the heck of it, she grabbed a few more and headed to the nearest armchair. As soon as she sat down and opened the first book she forgot where she was and almost why she was there.

It was a trick she'd learned in prison. Tillie had been an avid reader for years before landing up in the slammer, choosing to read a tattered copy of Are You There God, It's Me, Margaret or for the umpteenth time, A Wrinkle in Time. By the age of nine, sleep had already become her enemy. It deprived her of reading.

She learned to focus solely on the words until her ears blocked out the sounds of her mom fighting with yet another boyfriend. As a nineteen-year-old in the Dwight Correctional Institution, books served the same deafening purpose.

Tillie sat quietly, paging through a book on the original founders of Deadwood. The Harney name was prominent. Other names she recognized because of Hollywood movies or television series—Seth Bullock, Charlie Utter, Calamity Jane, Wild Bill Hickok and more.

The second book she'd chosen was bound in leather and regaled the gold rush era painted ladies. She scanned through the pages until one particular tintype image of an upstairs girl had her catching her breath.

The blurred black and white photo showed a determined young woman staring deadpan into the camera. Her face didn't reveal a single emotion, yet somehow her inner strength and determination was evident. In the caption below, the name Bella jumped out at Tillie.

"Bella Azzarello, twenty-two years of age." The date under the photo read 1876. Bella moved to the Black Hills as soon as the gold rush began.

Tillie studied Bella's ruffled skirt, notoriously short for the time, revealing the calf. A hint of a petticoat peaked from underneath. Her blouse too was of the same color, but over her shoulders she wore an embroidered fringe shawl. Tillie lifted the book to within inches of her eyes and studied the photo. Sewn into Bella's shawl were small bells.

The author wrote that in 1878 Bella married Hector Harney, a mercantile owner forty-three years her senior. Hector was Chad's great-great grandfather. The union produced three children. One of them was a girl who died at the age of seven from tuberculosis. The following year, her mother Bella died from the same disease.

That fact alone could explain why Bella's spirit hadn't crossed over. She was protecting her daughter, the one who left the disappearing palm prints on the attic's window. If Tillie could reach either one of them, perhaps was it was time for the two of them to leave.

The calico cat was sitting on another customer's lap, until she decided she was beyond bored. She leapt down with a clunk and headed toward Tillie. With precise jumping expertise she landed in the middle of

Tillie's lap. The driver adjusted the book in order to allow the cat to be both comfortable and within reach of constant petting. The two stayed in that position until closing time and Tillie was forced to leave. She'd sat absorbed in reading and didn't notice the time, or her hunger pains. Now with only a few minutes to spare, she couldn't decide which particular book to buy that she'd pulled from the shelf. Tillie decided to buy all of them. It was the same old, same old. Once a book was in her hands, it found a permanent home. At the register, Tillie ordered a bag of petit desserts to go.

"The total is ninety-five dollars and fifty-seven cents," declared the women who had welcomed her hours ago into the store.

Tillie handed her five twenties just as her phone began to vibrate. She decided to give the shop worker the courtesy of waiting until she stepped outside to check her messages.

"Here you go," the woman said, "Enjoy your books. We sell a lot of those books on the upstairs girls."

"Really?" Tillie asked, her interest rising.

"Half the folk around here like to say they're related to one, one way or another. A lot of that is poppycock, a bunch of wannabes. But, I swear on Wild Bill's grave that my great-great aunt was an upstairs girl. Of course that's before she became a prissy minister's wife. And a Baptist to boot!"

"Her name wouldn't happen to be..."

The clerk interrupted, "Harriet Lucia Barnes, same as mine."

Tillie smiled. She was hoping for a coincidental Bella connection. There wasn't one.

The sales clerk said, "Have a good night. Do you think you'll be gambling or hanging inside your hotel room to read?"

159

"Sort of gambling," Tillie answered. She avoided telling the clerk what she was really going to do. If she did, the woman would probably claim she was related to half the ghosts in the Black Hills.

Tillie stepped out on the porch and the deadbolt lock clicked behind her. She reached inside her favorite cell phone carrying case—her bra. There was only one text from Evan. It read, "Can't go exploring tonight."

There wasn't an apology attached or any explanation. And because she was leaving tomorrow afternoon, Tillie wondered if she'd hear from him again before the article was published.

His actions seemed rude, considering he'd spent half their previous encounter trying to lure her into his bed. And, knowing her own subconscious, she'd probably released enough pheromones to suggest to his testosterone that was actually quite a good idea.

And now he was bailing on her? And deserting Sarge? Unless it was some sort of an emergency, it didn't make sense. But the one thing she did know for sure, the actions of the men in her life rarely did.

TWENTY

The instant Codey hit Send on his cellphone he regretted it. The police station was only a short walk away. He could have talked to the Sheriff in person. Instead, standing on a sidewalk he'd texted, "Chad Harney hustler? Wyoming hooker? Hunch. Wyoming mentioned 'friend' owns nasty dogs."

If there were any connections to Johnson's murder and Chad, the sheriff would have surely discovered it by now. And if there weren't any, that meant Codey was slamming one of the most prominent and historic families of Deadwood based on a "feeling" he and his mom shared. For the first time since becoming a cop Codey felt like an amateur detective, and a bad one at that. He'd be lucky if the Harney family didn't sue the hell out of him.

Plus, his text would make no sense to the Sheriff, or at least the nasty dogs line wouldn't. Codey had failed to include the pertinent information that Wyoming's 'friend' was a hotel employee who procured her a room at a discount. And that she preferred staying at the hotel because of the canines. Did the sheriff even know Harney's animals appeared abused?

For years after texting became the norm, Codey refused to do it. He decided not only was it annoying but his fingers were too large to type on the little screens. Eventually he gave in, but he texted as little as

161

possible. He was right to be leery of all things smart phone related. Technology was useful, but as a cop, face-to-face worked better.

For a brief moment Codey thought of sending another message to explain his first, but decided against it. He slipped the phone into his pocket and decided to let the sheriff figure it out. Codey wanted to get out of his foul mood, or it would ruin the rest of his stay. He'd yet to find an engagement ring for Christine. Maybe if he spent the rest of the afternoon looking for the perfect ring for the perfect someone, it would make him feel his own imperfections less. He couldn't be that stupid, could he? If someone like Christine loved him? He scurried across Main Street and opened the door to Harney's.

The store was packed with customers browsing the shelves of tourist trinkets or gushing over the glistening array of jewelry. Fortunately, there were no young girls hanging around the section featuring engagement rings. Codey scuttled over to it. Below him, a dazzling display of Black Hills Gold rings, embedded with gemstones ranging from diamonds, rubies, opals and emeralds were present.

Two other clerks were working in the store, but it was Old Man Harney himself who walked to the other side and asked, "Can I help you?"

Codey answered, "I'm looking for an engagement ring."

"Are you interested in only an engagement ring or the complete bridal set?"

The expression on Codey's face explained he didn't have a clue what his answer should be.

Sounding irritated Harney asked, "Do you want to buy both at the same time, so they match? The engagement ring and the wedding ring?"

Codey shrugged. "Yeah, I guess."

"What about the groom's ring?"

Codey transformed into a non-responsive Neanderthal.

Harney explained, "The ring your fiancée will slip on your finger during the ceremony."

For that, Codey had an answer. "No, we're using my grandfather's ring."

Harney pulled out a black velvet tray of sparking bridal ring sets and set it on the counter. Codey scanned the three-dozen rings laid out in front him. There were so many designs to choose from, Codey almost walked away in frustration. Then he saw it. An engagement ring with a solitary 1-carat diamond set in the center, surrounded by green and rose leaves engraved into the 14k gold. The leaves on the wedding band intertwined, making the set appear as one.

He picked it up, studying it carefully; rotating it in his baseball glove sized hand. He said, "This one."

"Good choice," Harney answered. "Do you know her ring size?"

"Six," Codey answered.

"Perfect," Harney stated.

"She is," Codey replied.

Harney placed the tray back into the display case and pulled out a small velvet box. Codey reached out to hand the ring set back to the proprietor when a single gunshot boomed from the back of the store. The store's customers screamed and rushed toward the front entrance and out the door.

Without giving it a second thought, Codey raced behind the counter. Harney followed close behind. Stepping inside the back room, Codey reached for his gun. It wasn't there.

Dammit! Would he never remember he was on a holiday and that he wasn't armed?

Fortunately, there was no need for his weapon. Standing in front of him was a frail, octogenarian security guard. His trembling hand hung down at his

163

side grasping onto a Colt 45. The barrel pointed toward the wooden floor, directly over a small, smoking bullet hole.

Harney yelled, "For God's sake Ernie, haven't I told you not to put bullets in your gun?"

Ernie answered, "I thought with the lock being jimmied last night ..."

Harney interrupted, "I told you it was probably kids. Real burglars would have broken down the door."

Codey glanced around. An antique Mosler safe was positioned in the far corner. The only other items in the room were a table, a few chairs, and a refrigerator with a handwritten sign proclaiming, "It's my lunch, not yours."

Harney instructed, "Give me your gun Ernie. I'll put it in the vault in front."

Ernie handed him the weapon without bothering to check to see if the safety was on.

"Good looking safe you got back here," Codey stated pointing to the Mosler.

A look of fear crept into Harney's deeply wrinkled face. Codey realized he needed to put the man at ease. He said, "I'm a Chicago cop. I've seen a lot of those beauties in my time. They're absolutely gorgeous."

Harney relaxed. "Mosler, 1871. They don't get any better, than that. Well, except for the big safe upfront."

The guard asked excitedly, "Did someone break into those Mosler safes you were talking about? Were you investigating a burglary?"

"A few," Codey answered.

Ernie said, "I didn't know a Mosler could be broken into."

Codey responded, "If someone has the right tools they can usually break into anything, given enough time."

Harney shrugged off Codey's comment. He said, "It doesn't really matter if someone would break into

164

it. There isn't anything inside that safe that's worth anything to anyone, except me."

The security guard said, "You always tell me the stuff in the Mosler is priceless."

Harney answered bluntly, "To me." He turned to Codey and said, "Okay sir, let's wrap your up purchase."

Codey looked back at the antique safe one more time. Whatever was in it was Harney's business, even if he did call it both priceless and totally worthless at the same time.

∞

In less than twenty-four hours the Take a Chance tour would start its journey back to Chicago. Time was not only flying by, but questions were mounting about the consistently missing items being reported at Lame Johnny's, as well as the murder investigation.

Betty knew that the number one responsibility for a tour company owner was to make sure the hotels chosen were safe. The first time Take A Chance Tours stayed at Lame Johnny's, her office manager Gloria researched the hotel's history and safety rating. The establishment consistently rated five stars. There was no reason to think that had changed, even if the hotel did change owners.

Betty couldn't get Ester's missing house slipper out of her head. Of all the things that had been taken from the rooms, it seemed the silliest. A single house slipper? Who in the heck needed that? Even Hannah's George Washington troll could be rationalized as cute. Maybe the robber stole GW for his kid, and then had a change of heart so he returned it, puncture marks and all.

Behind the counter at Lame Johnny's check-in, a young woman was helping another guest. Betty waited patiently to speak with her. She felt it important to alert the hotel that Ester's slipper was taken from her room. Fortunately, she wouldn't have to deal with Chad. Not only was he unpleasant, but she feared she'd hurl one accusation after another at him. It was more than just that his animals appeared abused. It not only disgusted her that he was likely selling hooker services on the side, but his criminal activity could be even darker. It wouldn't be the first time a pimp killed a trick's "date".

Betty was a few feet away from the desk clerk when the sheriff and Chad rushed past. Chad led the sheriff into his office and slammed the door shut. Whatever Buckley wanted obviously didn't make Chad happy. But at this point in knowing him, Betty wondered if anything would.

She took two steps again towards the desk when Jerome called out to her from behind.

The seventy-six-year old caught up to her, gushing like a teenager. "You won't believe what happened!"

Betty said, "Something good, I hope." The last thing she needed now was for a client to claim another item had been stolen.

"More than good," Jerome answered, holding up a large flake of gold. If it weighed anything, it was less than tenth of an ounce.

Jerome continued, "Hannah and I went on that tour. They had us pan for gold and within ten minutes I found this little beauty sitting at the bottom of the pan. The tour host told me it's worth a hundred dollars."

"Not a bad profit," Betty added, remembering the tour only him cost twenty bucks.

"The guy said I could exchange it for money at Harney's, but I'm keeping it."

"Really?" Betty responded. She'd have thought most gamblers would have preferred the cash.

166

"Sure. I'm taking it to my grave with me. Figure that's the only way I can get my grandkids to visit." Jerome laughed and scurried off, stopping anyone who passed by to show off his discovery.

Chad's office door swung open and the two men stepped out. Buckley hurriedly left the building while Chad … Dammit! … replaced the woman at the front desk. Betty walked up to him gingerly.

"Good afternoon," Betty said in a terse monotone while remembering that '80s ad, Never let them see you sweat.

Chad didn't bother to ask if he could be of any help.

"I wanted to let you know one of my clients has reported another missing item…"

Chad began to sputter, "That's impossible. I made sure that she..."

He stopped in midsentence and his breathing became labored. It looked to Betty like he would hyperventilate at any given moment. She stood there, not saying a word. Every single one of her interactions with Chad bordered on the weird. This was the strangest one yet.

Finally, he was able to breathe normally. Through gritted teeth he asked, "What was taken?"

Betty answered, "It sounds silly, but a house slipper."

A look of relief came over Chad's face but the smile he gave her was little more than a smirk. He said, "Hold on."

Chad rushed to the other end of the reception desk. He rummaged around underneath the counter. When he came back up he was clutching a slipper in his hand.

Returning to face her directly, he asked, "Is this it?"

"I suppose it is,' Betty answered. "I mean I don't know the color, but how many single house slippers are out there? Can I ask, where did they find it?"

"One of our guests said it hit him on the head as he walked on the sidewalk in front of the hotel."

"Someone threw it at him?" Betty asked.

"No, he figures it slipped off of the balcony above him. It didn't hit him with any force. Who is the woman you are referring to?" Chad asked.

"Ester Hollenbridge," Betty answered. Poor lady. Chad would probably ban her too—this time for misplaced footwear.

Chad entered her name on the computer. "Hollenbridge is staying in a balcony suite on Main Street, directly above the area where the slipper landed. That proves it's hers."

Betty forced her lips tight against each, not allowing herself to yell, No it doesn't—or at least not in the forensic world of total accountability. There could still be other reasons. But Betty kept quiet. Odds were, after all, in Chad's favor.

He stated, "I'll have housekeeping return it."

Before Betty could say thank you, his attitude changed again from barely civil to repressed anger. He said, "My wife told me you stopped by our home to harass her?"

Betty sputtered back, "I wasn't harassing anyone! Besides, when I stopped I didn't know she was your wife."

Chad gripped the edge of the front desk firmly and asked, "Why did you stop?"

Betty answered, "To be honest, I was afraid she was fired because of me."

He shot back, "I'd never fire my wife."

It was pointless to argue with him, but she tried one more time to make him understand. "Once again, I did not know she was your wife until she told me."

His face muscles stiffened. "Then, how did you know where we lived?"

Betty said, "Finding your house was an accident. I was out for my morning walk and I came across Sasha drinking a can of beer in your front yard and..."

Chad interrupted, "—Beer? Sasha doesn't drink. She's in recovery."

Ah, no, she's not, Betty was wise enough not to say.

Chad said, "Like I said before, once you check out of the hotel, you're banned from ever stepping foot on a Harney property again. Try not to do anything else before that time to make me have the police arrest you for disorderly conduct."

Betty and Chad stormed off in different directions, leaving a trail of resentment behind them. Chad went back to his private office while Betty headed outside to cool down. Before their confrontation she was on her way to check out a fast food shop along Main Street that she'd read about on a foodie blog. After that, she planned on escorting a few of her passengers to the twilight historical stage reenactment of an old time shoot out on Main Street. Now she felt like she not only had participated in a shoot-out, but was the one who got shot.

Still, something interesting came of out her heated conversation with the hotel manager. Chad was convinced it was "impossible" something was taken again from a hotel room, because he made sure that 'she...' unfortunately he didn't finish his explanation. Betty had twenty-two hours, before she left town, to figure out what the hotel manager was implying and who this 'she' could be. Surprisingly, the time limit didn't concern her. Betty Chance solved far more baffling crimes in her past in way less time.

169

TWENTY-ONE

Mom, I can't believe what you're doing," Codey said, his voice resonating shock and awe.

Embarrassed, Betty set down the half eaten hotdog cradled in a sesame seed bun on the fast food counter. "You got me," she said sheepishly. "Sometimes I eat junk food."

"And not even high-end junk food, "Codey said, looking at the posted menu on the wall at Al's Aching Dogs. "What did that cost you? Ninety-nine cents for dinner?"

"Yes, but just because it's under a buck, doesn't mean it's not good. Actually, it's pretty great." She devoured another bite.

Codey motioned to the man at the window that he'd take two of the wieners and handed the man two bucks. Grabbing the still steaming frankfurters, he headed to his mom. Codey doused his purchase in ketchup before adding a layer of sweet relish. "You didn't want to eat at the buffet?"

"No reason to, I've already finished writing my review."

"Are you spending the evening with Tillie?" he asked, hoping she was, because he had plans of his own.

Betty said, "I don't know. Usually on a tour, we do spend a lot of time together. But Deadwood has her mesmerized. I have no idea what she has planned for the evening. What about you?"

Codey took a moment to respond. Not only was he mid-bite into chowing down, he wanted to be cautious with his answer. He didn't want his mom to know what he was going to do. If she knew, she'd insist on coming along, and that could be dangerous. Instead, he changed the subject.

He said, 'I didn't tell you I bought Christine's ring, did I?"

"That's wonderful! At Harney's?"

"I almost chickened out after the gunshot, but I figured what the heck, a great story for our grandkids."

Betty placed her hand on his forearm. "Wait a minute! Gunshot? Did someone shoot at you?"

Codey's attitude suggested it wasn't important. "Nah, not really. Harney's two-thousand-year old security guard managed to shoot the floor in the shop's back room. I was there at the time so I ran back to check out what was happening."

"How could he...?"

"I think he may have mistaken his weapon for a comb."

"That's not good."

"Never is. And, I believe it happened before."

"Did Harney take the gun away?"

Codey nodded. "He did, said he was going to lock it away in the big safe."

"Big safe? Does that mean he has a little one, as well?'

"From what I gathered, Harney's main vault is in the front area of the store. In the back room I noticed an antique Mosler."

"That had to be gorgeous."

"It was, all black and shiny, with a photo of a waterfall painted on the front. If there was rust, I couldn't see any."

Betty asked, "Speaking of ... did you leave Christine's ring in the safe back in your hotel room?"

171

"Nah," Codey answered. "I figured with what's been happening, it's safer with me." He unzipped his cargo pants pocket and pulled out a grey velvet box and handed it to his mom.

Once again Betty promised herself not to burst out into sobs, like some crazy, sentimental old lady. She didn't, not in sobs at least. Tears did fill her eyes as she opened the case. She managed to say, "The ring is absolutely lovely. Christine will love it."

Codey answered, "I hope so. But, she set the bar pretty low. Christine said she'd be happy with a pop can tab if it meant I'd marry her."

Betty handed the box back to Codey, and he placed it back in his pocket, zipping the pocket closed.

Codey asked, "What are you going to do?"

"After this fine meal, I'm heading back to Lame Johnny's to meet up with a few clients. I'm walking them to the twilight reenactment of a shoot-out on Main Street. Want to come along?"

"Maybe I'll catch up with you. I've got something I want to do first," He stood up to leave.

"Sounds good," Betty said as he walked away. Right before he opened the door, Betty yelled out, "And remember watch out for old men with combs."

Codey retorted, "Especially octogenarians."

∞

Sitting in the overstuffed armchair, Tillie opened the book on Deadwood's founding families and their lineage. Her normal reading habits consisted of mysteries ranging from humorous cozies to spine tingling serial killing tales. Now she wanted to familiarize herself with not only Bella's heritage, but any other spirit that might be hanging around. The

172

entire town seemed to be haunted with former citizens and ne'er do wells. It might be good to know their names.

She read to page three when the phone rang. She scooted to the nightstand and picked up the receiver.

"Hello," she said, half-expecting it to be Evan on the on the other end, saying he would join her tonight, after all.

No one responded on the other end.

Again Tillie said, "Hello?"

The line went dead. She headed back to the armchair but before she could reach it, ringing filled the room. She shuffled back again.

"You've reached Tillie," she said, slightly irritated. She waited for a response. None. She clicked the phone off and then pushed the button for the front desk.

An overly friendly female voice said, "Lame Johnny's. Can I help you?"

Tillie responded, "This is Tillie McFinn. Has anyone been calling my room?"

"Wait a minute..." the woman paused before adding, "not that I can see."

"Okay, no problem," Tillie answered and hung up the phone. There was only one soul who could be bugging her. She set the receiver back down into its cradle while her eyes scanned the room.

Tillie said, "Okay, knock it off. I know you're there. Either tell me who you are, or leave me the heck alone."

She walked back to her book and plopped down in the armchair and opened her book. As soon as her eyes fell on the word Bella, the phone rang again. She didn't pay the interruption any notice. She returned to her book and the words Bella and her daughter…

Ring. Ring. Ring

Tillie shut the book tight and asked cautiously, "Bella?"

173

Silence was the only response. Tillie realized she asked the wrong question.

She whispered, "Are you Bella's daughter? Who died at seven years old?"

A rush of cold air danced across her skin. Tillie suddenly felt the need to apologize, though she had nothing to do with any wrong that might have been done. She said gently, "I'm very, very sorry you died."

The windows to her room were closed, yet the sheer curtains swayed slowly back and forth.

Tillie asked quietly, "Is there something you need to tell me?"

No response. The phone didn't ring nor did the curtains move.

Tillie continued, "I get it, now. You went out on a little adventure and now you're lost. I bet you miss your mom."

The room shook slightly, but Tillie knew that could be from a semi that was driving by... still ...

"I know where your mom is," Tillie said and walked over to the window. She opened the window and a warm breeze danced about the room. Tillie pointed across the street and said, "She's in the attic at Harney's, waiting for you. You can fly through this window and go straight across the street, but first..."

The pale green sheer curtains stopped moving, as if pausing to listen.

"Tell your mom something for me, okay? Tell her it's time for the two of you to leave. She'll understand what I am saying."

The curtains moved again. Tillie knew it could be a coincidence, but she chose to believe that Bella's daughter had left the room. Tillie returned to reading, confident the phone wouldn't ring again.

TWENTY-TWO

Codey had little interest in watching a staged gunfight. It would be too much like going to work. Besides, he was more concerned on checking out the situation at the home of supposed dog abusers. Chad Harney's address was easy to find, once his name and city was entered into Google. Codey's street guide app on his smartphone showed the house was only a few blocks away.

He turned off of Main Street and ambled past retail buildings, the courthouse and the Adams Museum. He memorized the tourist sites with each step. The Black Hills would be a perfect honeymoon location. As he turned onto Harney's street, his GPS started flashing. The clapboard home was halfway up the block. His mom had mentioned the house was run-down. Either Chad was as cheap as his grandfather was known to be, or he didn't have time to take care of it.

Or—something else was going on.

Working in law enforcement, Codey had learned two things. If a house appeared to be perfect, not a speck of dust or a toy out of place, something was wrong. Living like that wasn't normal. At the other end of the spectrum, when a home was as disheveled and uncared for as Harney's appeared to be, and the family apparently had enough money to fix it, warning flags shot up that something was amiss.

Loud barking began when he was halfway down the block. The sound increased with every step. Codey stopped for a moment to ascertain the situation in front of him. A chipped, painted, picket fence surrounded the Harney yard. Two, agitated German Shepherds pulled angrily on their chains, while a small brown lab puppy raced back and forth. In the driveway a small moving van, its back doors opened, sat idling. Someone was home at the Harney estate, but they were getting ready to leave.

Codey decided to see what was happening. It was close to dark and more than likely he wouldn't be recognized as an interloper. The side door to the house opened and he crouched down, pretending to tie his shoe, glancing toward the house at all times.

Stepping out of the door was a woman who had to be Sasha. His mom was right. She should be on the cover of a magazine, not stepping out onto a rickety set of stairs, holding a beer can while an overnight bag hung from her shoulder. Sasha was slim yet voluptuous, with curves that were likely purchased at a plastic surgeon's office. Being a vice cop, Codey had seen her kind before—but usually it was sliding up and down a pole.

Sasha yelled, "Shut up you idiots" and threw the can at the dogs. The two immediately shut up and cowered in fear while the puppy chased the beer can.

Codey felt his anger rise as she continued down the steps. This time Sasha yelled, "Hurry up!" She hurried down the steps as the door opened again and a sloppily dressed blonde exited the house, followed immediately by the star of Dances with Wolves.

Codey recognized the man as being the reporter Tillie had been gushing over—the one she said was Costner's doppelganger. Rogers was supposedly writing an article about ghost hunting in Deadwood. But, he also appeared to be something else, Codey could recognize sinister a mile away, even if it looked like a Hollywood star.

176

The blonde wasn't a stranger to Codey. It was Wyoming, Nevada. This time she wasn't wearing a skintight dress or needlepoint high heels. She was dressed in an oversized gray sweatshirt with an image of Calamity Jane plastered across the front. Her black jeans were tattered, and her once upon a time white running shoes were scruffy.

Evan placed his hand firmly on Wyoming's shoulder and said, "Come on, get moving." He pushed her forward.

It wasn't yet technically abuse, but Codey could tell Wyoming was reluctant. If Evan ended up forcing her into the van against her will, Codey knew he'd have no choice but to leap up and come to her rescue.

Wyoming whined, "Do I have to go along, Sasha? I didn't sign up for this."

Sasha swirled around; her hands placed firmly on her hips. She spat out, "You knew exactly what you signed up for when you came back to Deadwood. I don't have time for your crap."

The two women walked toward the vehicle. Wyoming willingly climbed into the back, leaving the doors open. Sasha opened the door to the driver's side and bent over to step inside. As she did, Evan reached and swatted her behind. Sasha turned her head and Evan leaned in to kiss her.

She lifted herself into the driver's seat while Evan raced to the garage. He pulled up the single door and walked inside. Within seconds he carted two duffle bags out of the garage and tossed them in the back of the van. The moment the bags hit the floor, the sound of clanking metal emerged. As Sasha drove off, Codey could hear the song I Gotta Feeling escaping from the van.

At least the bastards have good taste in music, Codey mused as he walked over to share his pocket full of dog treats with his three new friends.

177

"Seven, eight … alrighty, you're all here." Betty lowered her index finger. Eight of her clients had signed up to head to the twilight shoot-out together. "Any questions before we leave?"

Hannah raised her tracing paper thin hand and asked, "Are the bullets going to be real?"

"No Hannah, not at all.

"Good, because with your track record…" Hannah stopped talking as soon as Betty gave her the all too familiar, say – one – more – word – and – you're - kicked - off - my - tours – for - good look.

Betty continued, "The bullets will be blanks and the men are all actors. But it's a really fun show and includes a little bit of history, humor, and a surprisingly accurate representation of what used to happen regularly on the streets of Deadwood."

Chuck added, "The Main Street shootouts are based on actual events and the firearms they use are from the gold rush era."

Betty said, "Plus their outfits are perfect replicas. You'll be in the spirit of the old west in no time."

Hannah asked, "Does that mean I'm going to feel like shooting someone?" Unfortunately, she wasn't kidding.

"I hope not," Betty answered. Knowing if Hannah did, it would probably be Betty that she'd be aiming at.

Jerome added a comment that surprised everyone connected with Take A Chance tours, including Hannah. He said, "Oh Hannah, you're too sweet to ever harm anyone."

Love is not only blind, Betty decided, it was also deaf and really, really dumb.

Betty announced, "Okay let's start trekking."

By the time they reached their destination on the street, Chuck had informed them, with every step he took, what they were about to see. He ended with, "We'll be watching the capture of the man who shot Wild Bill."

Betty added, "After that, those who wish can walk over to the Masonic Temple and watch a reenactment called The Trial of Jack McCall."

The streets were packed with tourists and families. Before the action started, the local actors walked up and down the street, deputizing small children. Chuck raised his hand to be chosen, but wasn't.

"Shucks," he responded.

When the action began, it only took ten minutes for the last shot to be fired and the reenactment to end. At the very last second, Betty felt a firm hand on her shoulder. The unexpected grasp made her jump.

Codey said, "Sorry mom. I didn't mean to scare you. I only wanted to let you know I was here."

"You're back early. I didn't expect to see you until later."

The crowd around them began to disperse.

Codey asked, "How long ago did you leave Lame Johnny's?"

Betty answered, "It took fifteen minutes to walk here, so maybe a half hour or less."

"Did you happen to see Chad in the lobby?"

"He was at the front desk when I left, sneering as usual. That guy must work twenty-four seven," Betty said before adding, "You were checking up on his dogs, weren't you?"

"Yeah, I happened to walk by his house."

"What do you think?"

"You were right, the dogs don't look very happy. And neither does his wife."

"You saw Sasha? Was she still drinking?"

179

Codey answered, "Let's talk about this after we walk your clients back to the hotel."

"Sounds good."

Codey asked, "Do you have plans for the rest of the evening?"

"No."

"I thought maybe we could go for a walk together."

"Okey doke," Betty answered, assuming she knew where her son was taking her—to confront the hotel manager's wife.

TWENTY-THREE

Two hours after reading about the lives of the Harney family and their descendants, Tillie's eyes sprang open. She'd fallen asleep cradling the leather bound edition in her arms. The clock radio was a glaring reminder that unless she put her butt in gear, she'd be late meeting Sarge and the rest of the tour.

Dang it!

One thing for sure, Bella's daughter had left the building. The phone hadn't rung in the last few hours and the room felt comfortably warm. The air was reminiscent of a stuffy old hotel room, not a whiff of lavender to be found.

A four-minute shower later Tillie tossed on her jumpsuit, tied her Nikes tight, and grabbed her backpack. Within seconds she charged down the hallway. The elevators brass doors slid open and Tillie squeezed inside. The small cubicle was packed with Take A Chance riders.

"Hey Tillie," Jerome greeted. "Heading downstairs to gamble?"

"Nope," Tillie answered cheerfully. "I'm going to the Bullock."

Hannah informed the group, "She's probably meeting up with that hunk again. She always does that, meets up with men."

Jerome asked, "You mean the guy who looks like that guy who starred in that movie?"

Chuck interjected, "People tell me I look like a movie star..." He paused for dramatic effect and possibly a drumroll before adding "Rin Tin Tin."

Except for Chuck, every single passenger let out a groan.

At the ground level Tillie stepped out of the elevator, waved goodbye and sprinted toward the exit. She raced down the sidewalks on Main Street. Her backpack moved up and down with every step, her red hair waving around her face, her Casper the Friendly Ghost earrings bouncing up and down.

Dark clouds rolled across the moon. A light rain had been predicted earlier, but from the looks of the sky a thunderstorm was brewing. As always, the streets were packed. Tillie's impromptu run was lit by street lamps and the glow of neon signs hanging in the casino windows. By the time she reached the exterior of the Bullock Hotel she paused to catch her breath.

Sarge was nowhere to be seen, nor were any other club members that she recognized. The group was supposed to meet at the front steps. She was only three minutes late. But then Sarge was ex-military. Perhaps he insisted on punctuality, even from his guests.

Tillie dashed into the Bullock's lobby hoping to see a familiar face. Instead, she was greeted by the whirl of slot machines, swirling cigarette smoke and tourists taking selfies. The Bullock was rumored to be the most haunted building in Deadwood. Tillie had been aching for years to go on a guided tour.

Maybe I can catch up, she decided. Sarge promised to take the group to room two hundred and eleven. Over a century ago, Seth Bullock passed away in it. Supposedly, his body was carried out of the room, but his spirit never left.

At the front desk Tillie said, "Excuse me."

The clerk lifted his head from a ledger and asked, "Can I help you?"

182

"Are you familiar with the Deadwood chapter of Ghost Hunters United."

"Sure am," the man replied.

"So, you probably know Sarge?"

The man flicked a piece of lint off his lapel and said, "Everyone knows Sarge.

"I'm late for the tour that Sarge is hosting. Do you know which part of the hotel he took the group to?"

The clerk lifted his index finger to give her the sign to hold on for a minute. He scanned the ledger in front of him. "Sarge called earlier and said the tour was cancelled."

Tillie mumbled, "Thank you," before stepping away, confused.

She reached deep into her cleavage and pulled out her cellphone. In her rush to get to the Bullock, she hadn't bothered to check her messages. Sarge must have sent a text while she was sleeping. She clicked it on but the last text was the one from Evan saying he couldn't make it. There was no implication in his message that the evening's outing had been cancelled.

"Well, that sucks," Tillie mumbled out loud, walking out of the building and slipping the phone back into her red lacy bra. At least the Chicago chapter of Ghost Hunters United would have had the courtesy to let her know a hunt was cancelled.

As usual, she decided to look on the bright side. There was one thing she had wanted to do, but if the tour went as planned she wouldn't have had time. Now she did. Perhaps it was fate intervening. It usually did.

She strolled Main Street through the throng of late night gamblers and tipsy cowboys who winked at her while she gifted them a coy smile in return. Passing by windows, she caught glimpses of slot machines or couples line dancing to live music. It was at the last casino, right before she planned to turn the corner, that she saw Sarge sitting at a video poker machine.

183

Tillie stopped abruptly, not knowing what to do. The man hadn't had the courtesy to let her know the tour was cancelled. But until this point, Sarge had been nothing except welcoming to her and kind. Perhaps part of Evan's text was deleted accidently. She needed to know.

Grabbing a tenner from her backpack, Tillie headed inside. She wanted to make it look like it was a coincidence she sat down next to him, possibly lessening the embarrassment on his part. Within seconds she was seated next to Sarge. His eyes focused on the Deuces Wild video poker in front of him, he didn't notice his new neighbor.

Tillie placed her cash into the slot, pressed play and said, "Oh! Hi, Sarge."

Startled, Sarge jumped before turning his head. He exclaimed, "Tillie! I guess you're feeling better."

His statement didn't make any sense. She felt great. Were Sarge's senior moments morphing into senior hours? She told him honestly, "I'm fantastic, have been since I arrived in South Dakota."

With a look of surprise Sarge said, "Evan texted me you were sick. Said you couldn't make it because you came down with a bug. He suggested I cancel the whole event."

"Nope, no bug here," Tillie said, not adding that she was beginning to smell a rat. Why did the reporter fib about her being sick? Was it that Evan didn't trust her to be alone with Sarge? Was there a chance she might discover something about the Dakota Daily reporter that he didn't want her to know? Or would his article on ghost hunters, and her in particular, be so cruel he couldn't bear to look any of them in the eye?

She asked, "Why do you think Evan said I couldn't make it tonight? Do you think he got a better offer?"

Sarge chortled. "Probably. He's always getting a bunch of top secret booty calls."

184

"Top Secret?"

"Yeah, he won't even tell me who she is," Sarge said and hit the play button again.

∞

"You don't mind walking in the rain without an umbrella?" Betty asked, stepping along the sidewalk, avoiding cracks in it.

"Nah, umbrellas are for wimps," Codey answered, pulling the hood of his rain jacket further down on his forehead.

Betty reminded him, "Your dad use to say the same thing."

"And then Dad kept getting these colds until he finally bought an ..." Codey didn't bother to finish. "I know you've told me a million times."

"Well, this will probably be the last time I do, so mark it down. From now on it will be Christine's job to keep you safe."

He laughed. "In a way, I'm more afraid of her then you."

"Good!" Betty teased. "That's the way it's supposed to be."

"Is there a specific place we're heading, or are you taking me along on your ten thousand steps."

"Both," she answered. "But first, did you check out the dogs at Sasha's?"

"They were in the front yard, like you said they'd be, chained to a tree."

"And Sasha?"

"She came out of the house as soon as I neared it."

185

"Did she notice you?" Betty asked, alarmed. Chad would probably try to have Codey arrested for stalking. Or worse.

"Nah, I was bending down, tying my shoe at the time."

"Ah, police surveillance 101." Betty said.

"She came out of the house swigging her last sip of beer, then threw the can at the dogs to shut them up."

Betty shook her head in disgust. "Unfortunately, it worked didn't it?"

Codey nodded. "Like a charm. They are terrified of her. But there's a lot more to the story."

Betty didn't know if she wanted to hear what else her son had to say. If he described more animal abuse, she wouldn't be able control her anger.

Codey continued, "Wyoming stepped out of the house immediately after her, and so did the reporter who's been hanging around Tillie."

It took Betty a second to digest Codey's statement and process what could be happening. She said, "Maybe Evan's an investigative reporter?"

"If he is, it involves kissing Sasha and smacking her rear in fun."

Wipe that option off the list, Betty decided. She said, "I don't think her husband would see the humor in that."

"Nope, and not only that, Sasha had a large overnight bag tossed over her shoulder. The three of them got into a small van, the kind someone rents when moving. To me, it looked like…"

Betty filled in her son's sentence "—Sasha's leaving her husband."

Codey added, "And Deadwood. And she's taking Wyoming with her."

A myriad of possibilities ran through her mind. From the look on her son's face, she knew he was doing the same game of mental aerobics.

186

Betty said, "I don't think Chad is Wyoming's pimp."

"Looks like it could be Evan."

"Or even Sasha," Betty added. Unfortunately, women could be as evil as men.

Checking the numbers on the houses they passed, Betty said, "It's at the end of this street. I found the address on this ..." Betty pulled out one of the hundreds of posters that had been plastered around town by the Sheriff's daughter. "I called the number listed on it and asked the woman who answered to stand in her front yard with the dog she found."

"Okay mom, I don't get exactly what your planning..."

"You will. Actually it was something you mentioned earlier that got me thinking. Remember when you said there was a puppy running around in Chad's yard."

"The chocolate Lab?"

"Sasha claimed Chad always had to have one dog named Bella, after his great-great grandmother...

"And?

"The puppy had to have a mother as well, correct?"

"Usually works that way," Codey added.

The two approached the pristine brick home. The sheriff's daughter waited on the front porch, the discarded adult chocolate Lab she'd found on the outskirts of town standing at her side. As soon as Betty and her son reached the end of the long driveway, Betty lifted her hands and yelled, "Bella, come here!"

The dog perked up its ears and ran across the water soaked front yard toward Betty, climbing up her torso, one muddy paw after another. Betty rubbed the dog's bobbing head and said, "Hello, Bella, you little thief. Good to finally meet you."

TWENTY-FOUR

The raindrops grew wider. Tillie kept her head down, the hood of her poncho covering her face. She maneuvered around puddles and past meowing alley cats. Earlier she yanked a thin, plastic rain poncho from her backpack. When folded in its pocket-sized carrier it measured only a few inches. Now unfolded it draped her upper body, keeping her completely dry. Not bad for a dollar investment at the dollar store, and perfect in case she'd ever be slimed by a spirit like in the movie Ghostbusters. So far, she hadn't.

Her hopes for the witching hour were polar opposite of what she normally hoped for when on a hunt. She didn't long to see a floating, luminescent orb shining through the window, or catch a glimpse of a child's palm print pressed against the glass. She only wanted to know that Bella and her daughter had left planet earth, and that of course, meant no sighting at all.

Nearing the back of Harney's Tillie finally lifted her head. It was five seconds before she breathed again.

The two doors on the loading dock to Harney's were standing wide open. Through the mist, a yellow light filled the space. Standing dead center of it was a woman in red. The glowing aura from the evolving thunderstorm made visibility difficult, even in such close proximity. Tillie was fixated on the vision in front of her and failed to notice the vehicle parked in front of the loading dock.

Bella was slimmer than Tillie thought she would be, and taller. Her hair was a deep brunette and her... What the heck? Bella was wearing skinny jeans? And a black bra that peeked through opened buttons? Did they even have push-ups during the gold rush?

Tillie had walked smack dab into the middle of a robbery at Harney's. She turned and started running on the slippery pavement. She managed to make it twenty feet or so before a set of muscular arms wrapped around her and dragged her back to the idling van.

A male voice whispered in her ear, "What the hell are you doing here?"

"Evan?" she questioned, hoping he was rescuing her. But instead, the reporter dragged her toward the pouting woman in red.

Sasha looked down from the loading dock and said, "You're that bus driver aren't you? The loony one who believes in ghosts."

Tillie spat out, "You're robbing a store and you're calling me looney? Don't you see the security cams all around you?"

Sasha answered, "They're fake, I bet. You think my father-in-law would actually pay for real cameras to be installed?"

"Father-in-law?" Tillie asked. "You're Sasha, aren't you? The hotel manager's wife? Betty told me all about you."

Sasha spat. "Your boss doesn't know anything about me. She thinks I'm happy being a stupid maid."

Evan said, "We have to finish and get out of here. What do I do with her?"

"Grab her backpack and toss it to me. She may have a phone they can trace."

Evan yanked Tillie's backpack off and threw it to Sasha, who tossed it on the floor.

Tillie yelled, "Hey, be careful!"

Sasha ignored her. "Evan, tie her up and leave her in the van, next to Wyoming."

Evan said, "Are you sure? We don't want another Johnson situation on our hands."

Alex Johnson? Evan and Sasha were the killers?

Sasha instructed, "I'm sure. We'll decide what to do with her when we get there."

"Tie her up with what?" Evan asked, looking around. "We didn't exactly plan for this."

A tiny voice from inside the van said, "There's a few bungie cords lying on the floor."

Evan pushed Tillie into the vehicle so hard she fell on her face. She leaned up and whispered to him, "Please tell me you're an undercover reporter."

He pulled her up off the floor and forced her to sit on the bench seat next to Wyoming. Grabbing the cords, he wrapped them around Tillie's wrists and ankles, tying them into knots in the process. He leapt out and returned to the dock.

Wyoming leaned over and whispered, "Sorry, but I was afraid he'd remember he had duct tape in here. I knew you wouldn't like that."

I'd like it better than this, Tillie thought. If applied in a certain way duct tape was something she could easily escape. YouTube had shown her how. Now, she made a mental note if she ever got out of this, she'd search for Escaping from Bungee Cords 101 on YouTube's innumerable survival channels.

Evan headed back to the loading dock, and knelt in front of an old safe. The sound of a power drill began as metal sparks flew into the air.

Tillie said, "You're Wyoming, Nevada aren't you?"

Wyoming held her head low.

Tillie recognized the symptoms of immediate regret. Not only had she felt them herself, but during

190

her decade in prison, learned to identify them in others. It was the one way she knew how to survive, to attach herself to others who yearned for redemption.

The drilling stopped. Evan pushed something inside the hole he just drilled. Using his Bic lighter he set, what looked like a cord on fire. He and Sasha ran as far back as they could. Suddenly, a loud boom filled the air and the front door fell open. Evan waved his arms to clear the smoke. He reached into the safe and yanked out a single piece of paper.

"Got it," he announced.

Sasha and Evan bolted off the dock. Evan slammed the van's back door shut and rushed into the driver's spot to start the van. Sasha climbed into the passenger seat, turning on the overhead light in the process. She studied the yellowish piece of paper as Evan tore down the alley, smashing into trashcans along the way.

Sasha yelled, "Dammit, Evan. Be careful."

He didn't respond, but kept his eye on the rearview mirror as if cop cars would be honing in on him at any second.

"Where does it say to go?" he demanded.

Sasha whined. "I don't know. I can't figure it out. I've never been good at reading friggin' maps."

Tillie popped her head up and said, "I am."

Sasha growled, "Shut up."

"No really, I'm a professional bus driver and..."

Sasha said, "Wyoming, hit her."

Wyoming didn't move a muscle but instead slumped down as if hit by a tsunami of depression. She mumbled, "No."

Sasha swirled her head around and hissed, "You'll pay for not listening to me.

The young woman managed to snipe back, "I already have."

Good! Tillie thought. The escort could easily be convinced to come over to her side, perhaps even help her escape.

Evan yelled with full force, "Sasha, where do I turn? I can't keep speeding through alleys."

Sasha lifted the map to within inches of her face. She answered, "I don't know. Turn on Main Street."

At the same time, Evan and Tillie said, "That's stupid."

Sasha said, "Okay, then keep driving north until I can figure this out."

He growled, "Aren't there any side streets?"

Tillie scooted a few inches toward Wyoming and asked, "Do you know what Sasha's holding?

Wyoming answered, "A treasure map..."

Tillie asked, "Like a pirate's treasure map?"

"Lame Johnny's."

So that's what Harney kept locked away in his safe. No wonder the rumors claimed he was the richest man in the Dakotas. Then it hit her, the gold nugget found in Harney's attic could be part of Lame Johnny's bootie. The map may actually be real, and if it was, Harney may have carted the treasure away a long time ago.

Tillie yelled, "You actually think Harney hid a map that will lead you to fourteen million dollars in lost gold?"

Sasha spit out, "If you knew my father-in-law like I do, that little fact wouldn't surprise you. Harney wouldn't share a dime with himself, much less anyone else."

Tillie decided Sasha was not only delusional, but she'd convinced Evan and Wyoming to go along with her hallucinations. At the moment, the best thing Tillie could do was to jump on the insanity train. She said, "Remember how you said Betty didn't know everything about you ..."

192

That caught Sasha's attention. Tillie could see her looking at the rearview mirror. "Here's something you, or Evan the great reporter, don't know about me. I'm a convicted felon."

Evan said, "Your mug shot's all over the Internet."

"Oh, never mind" was all Tillie could say in response.

Sasha added, "It's not a very flattering one. Even my husband laughed at it."

"Why did you show your husband? Is he in on this too?" Tillie wanted to get as much information as possible. If Chad were involved, it would be good to know.

"I figured he'd like to know who was staying at the hotel."

Evan asked, "Any damn idea where we're heading?"

Sasha said, "I can't figure it out. I don't know, north of town ..."

Tillie interrupted..."—Again, I am excellent with reading a map."

"And why should we trust you?" Sasha asked.

"Because if I help you find fourteen mil, I figure you'll give me a reward," Tillie lied. Or kill me, like you did Johnson, she thought.

Sasha handed Wyoming the map. She said, "Hold this up to Tillie's face. Let's see if Miss Brainiac can figure it out."

TWENTY-FIVE

Betty dropped the paperback in her lap when the knocking started. Her latest Jessie Chandler read would have to wait. As soon as she heard the word Mom, she dashed to the door.

Standing outside in the hallway Codey asked, "Did you hear an explosion?"

Betty nodded. "A boom or something. I was hoping it was fireworks."

Codey explained, "Harney's been robbed."

"The store?"

"The employee break room in the back of the store. Someone's broken into the safe."

"And...?" There had to be more to the story, otherwise Codey wouldn't be knocking on her hotel room door at midnight.

"Tillie's involved..." He paused before adding, "...somehow. The sheriff called. He wants both of us there immediately."

Betty grabbed her shoulder bag and said, "Let's go."

Mother and son dashed to the end of the hallway and down the emergency stairwell. There was no time to wait for an elevator. As soon as they hit the lobby level they raced past dozens of hotel guests whose faces were pressed against the glass, peering through the pouring rain outside. They ran across the street without looking. There was no need to worry about

194

traffic. Sawhorses draped with crime tape stood at the ends of the block.

Hundreds of gawkers gathered on the sidewalk in front of the store. The two pushed their way through the throng of tourists and headed to the front entrance. Aware of their pending arrival, a police officer allowed them to enter without asking who they were.

Codey indicated Betty to follow him down the hallway leading to the back of the store. They stopped when they reached the combination employee break room and loading dock area.

Betty could see across the space to the alley. At the end of the room, the double doors were opened wide. In the middle of the room, Buckley stood near a table where employees normally sat. But now it was littered with items taken from Tillie's backpack. Betty recognized the driver's make-up bag, bottle of Aqua net hairspray, EMF meter and wallet. The backpack was in the Sheriff's hand.

The sheriff said sternly, "Chance."

Betty and her son walked up to the table and at the same time answered, "Yes?"

Betty realized her mistake and took a step back. This was her son's territory, not hers.

Buckley announced, "We found this backpack near the safe."

He tossed the empty bag onto the table and Betty gasped. The exterior of the backpack was shredded. Holes were ripped into the leather and the straps were torn from their base. If Tillie had been wearing the backpack when the explosion happened, she might have been killed. Betty's eyes scanned the area again, as if to catch sight of her closest friend sprawled on the floor, her body outlined by chalk.

Codey placed his hand on Betty's shoulder and asked, "Mom, is that Tillie's?"

"Yes, and those are her things."

The sheriff lifted up a small bottle and asked, "What's this?"

Betty answered, "SpiritsBGone is used to, well, chase spirits away."

When the sheriff didn't respond, Codey asked him, "What's Tillie's connection to this? Besides the pack? You're not implying she blew-up the safe, are you?"

"Not at all," the sheriff said, motioning for them to follow.

The sheriff led them to Harney's office where a video monitor replayed the explosion captured by a security camera.

Betty stammered, "I, I thought the store's cameras were fake. They look so…" Betty paused, not knowing if she should continue on with her critical description.

Buckley finished her sentence for her. "—Cheap? A lot of the new cameras are built to look that way. The reasoning is that if a crook wants to break in, they will. And, if they don't think a camera will record their faces, they don't bother to hide them."

The sheriff picked up a remote and pressed Rewind. The recording skipped backwards to 12:01 a.m., a few minutes before the explosion. He hit Play.

Though her face wasn't visible, Betty recognized the woman standing at the edge of the dock. Sasha. The image of her backside was crystal clear, but unfortunately there was no audio. The two people standing on the ground looking up were easily visible. Evan stood behind Tillie, one arm wrapped around her in a chokehold, while his other gripped her left arm. Betty moaned and her stomach hit rock bottom. She became woozy and grabbed onto Codey for support. He immediately wrapped his arm around her shoulder, helping her to keep standing.

The recording continued playing and Betty watched as Evan pushed Tillie into the back of the van.

196

Both of them disappeared from the image on the monitor.

"We don't know for sure, but we think Evan is tying Tillie up in the back of the small moving van. Sasha rented the vehicle earlier today in Rapid City."

Evan's image returned to the monitor and he jumped up on the loading dock. Sasha's face appeared the moment she turned around to pick up a bag of tools from the floor. She handed it to Evan, who kneeled in front of the safe.

The sheriff stopped the recording and said, "I think they've taken Tillie."

"As a hostage?" Betty asked.

'Or simply because she was a witness," the sheriff responded.

Codey asked, "How much money did they get?"

"Not a penny," Harney interrupted, entering the room. On his head sat a fedora and his trench coat was buttoned. He'd obviously just arrived. Harney edged his way to his desk, sat down and said, "Sasha's always been a greedy idiot. From the moment my son married that drunk stripper, I knew they'd have problems."

Stripper? Was Sasha a stage name too, like Wyoming's moniker? And if they both were erotic dancers at one time, Sasha might certainly be Wyoming's pimp.

"What was in the safe, Harney?" Buckley asked. "Jewels, gold…?"

Harney sat down at his desk. "Not a damn thing, except an April Fool's gag!"

Betty couldn't stop herself. "My friend's life is in danger and you're making a joke?"

Harney started to explain, "I'm talking about a real April Fool's joke, made a long time ago when I…" He stopped speaking, trailing off into silence.

197

This time it was Buckley who hollered. "Harney! Someone's life is in danger. Explain yourself."

Old Man Harney breathed deeply and began, "At fifteen years of age, I fell in love with the most beautiful girl in Deadwood, Cindy Caulfield. She didn't know I was alive. Then one day she passes me a note, asking me to meet her after school."

Buckley demanded, "Get to the point."

Harney said. "That afternoon she gave me an old, handwritten treasure map with a red X in the middle. She told me Lame Johnny's gold was hidden in a partially dug water well that was eight feet deep. Her grandfather stopped digging when he discovered the gold."

Harney said, "And she asked you to retrieve it?"

"At dusk. She claimed she wanted to move to Hollywood and I could go with her. I was to start digging as soon as I got there."

"And you believed her?" Betty asked.

Harney answered, "There was no reason not to, not with those eyes. Besides I was only fourteen. In those days, I believed everyone."

Buckley explained, "Unfortunately, this kind of story has happened before around here. I'm guessing Harney showed up, climbed down using a rope that was conveniently lying on the ground, tied to a tree...

Harney interrupted, "And as soon as I reached the bottom of the well, Cindy and her friends arrived and pulled the rope up."

"Trapping you." Betty grimaced.

Harney continued, "Cindy and her three friends, looking down the well and laughing at me. Cindy yelled, 'April Fool'. They left me like that. It took me two days to climb out of the pit."

Betty uttered, "That was their April Fool prank?"

Harney continued, "It was, but it taught me the most important lesson in my life, and the reason I kept

198

the damn fake map. I eventually bought the damn land surrounding the well and left it as it was, as a further reminder. Never trust anyone you love, not even for a second."

That explained the family dynamics in the Harney family—an entire life of misery and distrust caused by a bunch of middle school bullies.

Codey asked, "Your daughter-in-law didn't know it was a joke? She heard about its existence from Chad and thought the map was real?"

Harney answered, "I let both of them think that. I figured Chad would tire of her yammering on and on about how wealthy they could be if they only had the map."

Buckley said, "And you think Sasha's looking for Lame Johnny's fortune?"

Harney answered, "Yes, and I can tell you exactly where she's heading."

∞

Sasha sneered at Tillie. "I may not be good with reading a map, but I'm great with distance. If we're not at the site in fifteen minutes, we're kicking you out of the van."

Tillie lifted her head from studying the piece of parchment and asked, "And I wouldn't like that, because…?"

"We're not stopping when we do it," Evan answered.

Tillie went back to the map and announced, "Turn left on Potato Creek Road and drive approximately three miles."

The location was easy enough to find, but Tillie had already decided the supposed treasure map had to be a fake. The parchment appeared old, but the same look could easily be accomplished by soaking the paper in tea for a few seconds. The ink was black and smudged. A large X appeared to be drawn in red crayon. How many outlaws took out their box of Crayola's to chart their course?

Tillie asked, "Wyoming, let me see the back of the map."

Wyoming turned over the paper and held it close to Tillie's face. Tillie's hands were still bound with the bungee cords. But, her feet were moving frantically to loosen the cords from her ankles. If nothing else, she might be able to bolt when the doors opened. Wyoming noticed Tillie's ankle actions, but didn't say a word about it.

"Why in the hell do you want to look at the back of the map?" Sasha sniped.

"Leave her alone, Sasha," Evan shouted. "She's helping us."

"Huh," Sasha scoffed while reaching into the glove box to grab a can of beer. She snapped it open and began to glug.

Evan said, "Give me one."

Oh great! Tillie thought sarcastically, this ride just keeps getting better and better.

Tillie announced, "It's against the law to drink and drive."

Sasha shot back, "And it's against the law to kill you, but that doesn't mean I won't."

Tillie knew she was taking a chance when she asked, "Like you killed Johnson?"

Sasha retorted, "I didn't kill him. He ..." She didn't finish her sentence. She didn't need to. Tillie realized then Johnson's death wasn't intentional, but Sasha did have a hand in it somehow. And if Tillie weren't careful, Sasha would have a hand in hers.

Tillie returned to analyzing the back of the map. It took only a few seconds to decipher the simple code written in at the bottom to confirm what she suspected. She said, "Turn on Buffler's Road next, and drive for exactly half a mile until you come to a one lane gravel road on your left. Don't turn on it but stop the van. The treasure will be buried one hundred yards on your left."

TWENTY-SIX

In the rearview mirror, Betty watched as the town of Deadwood disappeared. Codey convinced Buckley to allow his mother and him to ride along in the squad car. The sheriff gave in easily, assuming either Tillie would need a shoulder to cry on, or by the look on Betty's determined face, the woman would show up at the site anyway. Old Man Harney had given clear and precise directions, as if he'd been there a hundred times since 1946.

The sheriff asked, "Betty, do you have a cell?"

She yanked the phone from her purse. The lit up screen caught her eye. "I have a message!" She squealed before her spirits plummeted. The text wasn't from Tillie.

"It's from Wyoming!" Betty informed him.

The sheriff asked, "What did she say?"

"She sent 'please help me get out of here'."

"When was it sent?" the sheriff questioned.

"Four hours ago."

From the front seat, Codey said, "That was before the robbery. It sounds like she's terrified."

Betty interjected, "And wanted out."

Buckley said, "She's probably in the van as well. Call Tillie. Do you know if she keeps her phone on?"

"Usually, but it's on vibrate." Betty didn't bother to explain Tillie liked the way it felt against her boobs every time a call or a message arrived. Or the fact that Tillie considered her cleavage to be the perfect hiding place for all things portable.

202

The sheriff responded, "Even better. Text her the words 'Hello, how are you tonight?' Don't write anything else. Let's see if she responds."

Betty clicked on her cell and typed the words the sheriff suggested and hit Send. Her words alone would show Tillie her rescue was imminent. Betty never once sent a stiff, formal text like that to her dear friend.

She waited for a minute before announcing, "She didn't respond." Without the sheriff suggesting it, Betty pressed Send over and over again. If for no other reason, she wanted to assure Tillie she was thinking of her.

Codey asked, "How long till we get there?"

"Ten minutes max." The sheriff pressed the gas pedal harder.

Betty leaned forward to see the speedometer. The squad was going at sixty miles an hour up and down narrow, winding mountain roads. Two other squad cars followed close behind.

Codey said, "I'm thinking Sasha is Wyoming's pimp."

Buckley answered, "We're sure of that."

"Really?" Codey replied.

Betty wanted to yell so why didn't you friggin arrest her earlier? If the sheriff had, perhaps Johnson would be alive and Tillie wouldn't be held hostage. But, she knew to keep her opinions to herself. It wasn't as if the Sheriff hadn't already thought of that possibility. More than likely he was beating himself up for that very decision.

Buckley said, "You don't wear Jimmy Choo shoes when you're working as a maid."

Wow, the Deadwood sheriff was a fashionista! Who'da thunk? Betty mused bitterly, knowing her twisted sense of humor got the best of her, even in the worst of times.

Buckley admitted, "We were trying to see if her husband was involved, and Old Man Harney himself. Now, we're convinced it was only her."

"Not Evan?" Betty asked.

Buckley responded, "Nah, he's just another angry, underpaid reporter. Plus, having a gambling addiction doesn't help. The man's bounced checks at every casino in a four state area."

Betty said, "I thought he wrote for the Dakota Daily."

Buckley answered, "He does, but only freelance. One hundred bucks an article."

That was still more than Betty made writing her blog and she'd yet to break into a safe.

Buckley continued, "Besides Evan's madly in love with Sasha, emphasis on the word mad."

Betty asked, "What about Johnson?"

Buckley said, "Oh, Sasha was certainly involved in his death. We were waiting for the DNA evidence to prove it. Even though the old man hates her, the Harneys are still a powerful family in this state." The sheriff lifted his hand and pointed toward a dirt road, a quarter of a mile ahead. "That's where we're turning."

Buckley didn't slow down as he made the turn and Betty slid halfway across the seat, even with her seat buckle strapped.

∞

The thunderstorm was in full force as the van came to a screeching halt, sending mud and gravel into the air. The wind rustled through the Ponderosa pines and white flashes danced across the sky. The electrical jolts were closer with every passing second. Tillie counted,

"One Mississippi, two Mississippi, three …" Boom! Rats! The strikes were less than a mile away.

Evan turned off the car. "Now what?"

Sasha said, "Grab the shovels."

Evan responded, "You've got to be kidding me? We're using metal shovels during a lightning storm?"

Sasha pointed toward the back of the van. "Not us—those two."

Wyoming and Tillie looked at each other as if recognizing that both their lives were up for grabs.

Tillie said, "Again … professional bus driver here? Hello? Trust me, I know weather patterns. This storm will be over in a few minutes."

It wouldn't be, but Tillie was trying to stall. The fact that her phone vibrated for five minutes straight meant someone was trying to get ahold of her. If she was lucky, her backpack was found at Harney's and the police were tracking her phone.

Sasha rolled down the window and tossed an empty can out into the dark and then clicked on the sound system. I Got a Feeling raced through the speakers.

Evan asked, "Again? We've been listening to that all day."

"It's my good luck song," she responded. "Besides, Oprah likes it."

Evan tossed his beer can out the window and pointed at the glove box.

Another beer? Now? Tillie cringed at the thought of Evan driving drunk. But it wasn't a Coors that she handed to Evan. But it was just as bad—a Beretta handgun.

Tillie needed to be able to judge Evan's potential for violence. She whispered to Wyoming, "What happened to Johnson?"

At the moment, Tillie could care less about Johnson. She wanted to know her odds in surviving the situation. If Sasha's anger had gotten the better of her once before and it caused a man to die, she could easily be that careless again. And if Evan were involved, now that he had a gun in his hand, Tillie's chances for living decreased at an alarming speed.

Wyoming admitted, "Johnson fell."

"How?"

"Sasha shoved him and he slipped backwards. His head hit the faucet."

That had to be some push!

But, it was an easy one for Tillie to visualize. For whatever reason, Sasha slammed into the man with rage and Johnson tumbled into the whirlpool. But, Johnson was a big guy. Someone had to help Sasha arrange the body so that it appeared to be a suicide.

"Why?"

Wyoming answered, a catch in her throat as if she were about to burst into sobs. "Sasha threatened to blackmail him, but he refused to break into the safe. Sasha said it would have been easy for him to do because he was a locksmith."

"Did you help her move the body into the tub?" Tillie asked as Evan stepped out of the van.

"I wasn't there, yet, but ..." She stopped talking as soon as Evan opened the back door. Aiming the gun at Tillie, he motioned for Wyoming to untie her.

Tillie looked to see if there was anything she could grab to use against Evan. A claw hammer was sticking out of a tool bag, along with a power drill. She calculated her chance of being able to grab the hammer and hit Evan on the head before she was shot.

Not one in a million.

For now, it was fruitless to resist. Tillie allowed Wyoming to untie her wrists and ankles without resisting. As the final cord came off, Wyoming looked up at her and said, "I'm sorry."

The women climbed out of the van, Tillie's feet sinking into the mud.

Evan said, "Grab the rope, Tillie."

Tillie scanned the area and saw a coil of rope. She picked it up and slipped her arm through the loop and allowing her shoulder to carry the weight of the coil.

Evan said, "Now the shovels!" Tillie grabbed one and handed the other to Wyoming.

"Take me to the spot," Evan instructed.

Tillie asked, "Do you have a flashlight? I won't be able to see anything without one." The moment she finished speaking, a bolt of lightning struck the ground nearby. The thunderstorm's intensity was increasing by the second as the wind rushed through the trees.

Still holding the Beretta, Evan reached into the van and pulled out a small, handheld spotlight. Tillie recognized the brand from nights spent ghosting in rural cemeteries. The brand could light up a coyote at forty yards.

Evan demanded, "Which way do we go to find the X spot?"

Tillie's mind whirred at full speed. Her eyes scanned the area, looking for an escape route. There wasn't any, yet. Briefly she considered admitting to Evan what she discovered on the back of the map. If she did, perhaps they'd all share a good laugh and call it a night.

Not likely.

"That way," Tillie answered, pointing towards a gigantic Ponderosa pine.

Think! Think! Think! Tillie repeated to herself as the three of them walked toward the hillside, while Sasha sat in the van, fiddling with her fingernails. Instantly, the area in front of Tillie lit up. Sasha had managed to pause long enough from her manicure issues to turn on the van lights to help guide their way.

Tillie pointed, "There, in the distance. Do you see that? The old boards piled up on the ground?"

Evan said, "Keep going."

Tillie and Wyoming trudged through the mud and rain. As soon as they reached the discarded lumber, Tillie said, "We have to move the wood out of the way."

"Then do it," Even demanded.

Tillie turned her helpless, and oh so feminine ploy on. "But it's heavy and I don't know if I can..."

"Don't give me any lip," Evan reacted.

Okay, Plan A didn't work. It involved having Evan help to move the planks while she quickly picked one up and knocked him out cold. Now for Plan B and if that doesn't ... how many more letters were in the alphabet? Oh yeah, twenty-four. A heck of a lot of plans.

Tillie tossed the rope to the ground and warned, "Wyoming, be careful. A deep well hole underneath this wood was drawn on the map."

"Thanks," Wyoming answered.

The van horn tooted behind them. Sasha leaned out the window and loudly asked, "Did you find it?"

"Not yet," Evan shouted back. "Any second."

Tilled picked up one end of the plank while Wyoming grabbed the other. They tossed the wood, piece by piece, to the side. When the last board was lifted, a crude circular opening appeared in the ground. Tillie had no idea how deep the well was, or if there was water sloshing about at the bottom. The one thing she knew for sure, there wasn't any gold to break her fall.

TWENTY-SEVEN

Watch out!" Betty screamed, her torso yanked forward as the sheriff hit the brakes. The squad CAR skidded sideways on the slippery mountain road to a complete halt. The two police cars behind did the same.

Codey uttered, "What the…?"

A lightning strike illuminated a herd of Bighorn Sheep crossing the road in front of them, slowly.

"How much do those things weigh?" Betty asked, while trying to catch her breath. If the sheriff had rammed into the animals, not only would the car have been destroyed, it would have ended up careening down the side of a cliff.

"Close to three hundred pounds. Just be happy it's not bison. We'd be stuck here forever."

Well, not forever, but long enough that they might not be able to save Tillie.

The sheriff said, "We'll have to wait it out. If I turn on the siren, they might start ramming the squad."

As long as she was stuck sitting in South Dakota's version of a traffic jam, Betty decided to ask, "Was Sasha the one stealing from the guests, and from the town's residents?"

The sheriff answered, "No, that was Bella." At that moment the last Bighorn disappeared and Buckley hit the gas pedal. Betty would have to wait to ask him to explain his answer. With one hand, she grabbed the doorframe as the other grasped the seat cushion and held on. But no matter how scary it was to be riding in a car speeding at night in the Black Hills in a thunderstorm, she realized Tillie's fear level was even higher.

∞

The raindrops turned into pellets and slammed into Tillie's face. She lifted her hand to wipe the cascading water from her eyes.

Standing on the other side of the well hole, Evan demanded, "Don't move!" He held the Beretta in one hand, and the spotlight in the other.

Tillie responded, "My mascara's running, it's getting into my eyes." Her hair was drenched and the taste of Aqua Net dribbled onto her lips. She moaned at the thought that her corpse would look like an extra on The Walking Dead.

Evan answered, "Don't care."

"You won't actually shoot us, will you?" Tillie pleaded.

"Shut up," Evan reiterated.

Again? Shut up? For a man of words like Evan supposedly was, he used only a few.

Tillie continued, "Listen, as an ex-con, shooting us makes no sense. You did what? Steal a piece of paper? Blow up an old safe? The most they'll give you is community service."

Evan didn't move a facial muscle.

Tillie continued, "And if you're worried about a kidnapping charge, how are they going to prove it? It's not the first time I've driven off in a van with some man. Your lawyer would have a field day with my background."

Evan responded, "You know, I think I'll pull the trigger just to get you to stop talking."

Tillie complied. Whatever charm she'd once used on Evan had evaporated. She'd have to use a different tactic to save her life. If she could get close enough, maybe she'd be able to try one of the self-defense moves she'd learned at the YWCA, or better yet, she'd use the one skill she mastered that wowed her classmates in fifth grade. One she learned watching reruns of her favorite TV show.

Evan turned his head slightly as he yelled to Sasha, "Turn the van around!"

Leaning out of the passenger's side window Sasha asked, "Why? You know I hate driving stick."

Evan demanded, "Put it in reverse and drive it slowly backwards to where I'm standing. The van's too far to carry the gold."

"Fine, but I'm not happy about this. Poor planning on your part." Sasha stepped out of the van. She began to walk around it to the other side, cursing as her high heels made three-inch holes into the mud with every step.

The spotlight lit up the vertical tunnel, and Evan instructed Tillie, "Get in."

Tillie asked, "How? Jump? I'll break my leg, then what good would I be to you?" Not only was it a long drop, but rocks, empty and broken whiskey bottles, beer cans, and whatever else kids tossed down a hole when they wanted to hide evidence of partying, waited at the bottom.

Evan said, "Use the rope to climb down. Tie the rope around the tree behind you."

Tillie said to Wyoming, "I'll do it." She assumed Evan's plan was to have her and the escort lift Lame Johnny's gold out of the hole, bag by bag.

As she turned to walk, she heard the van behind her start and then stop, then start and stall as the gears ground against each other.

Tillie only knew two knots. One was a bowline. She used it to secure the rope around the tree trunk. The loose end she frantically tied into the Honda knot. Fortunately, the name had nothing to do with cars. She knew there was a strong chance that Plan B would fail miserably, and that she, or Wyoming might be shot in the attempt.

She walked back clutching the loose rope in her hand and determined to see if telling the truth would work. "Before we climb down, there's something I need to tell you."

Evan asked, "What now?"

"The map's fake."

Evan scoffed, "Good try. I'm not buying it."

Tillie said sternly. "Didn't you notice the writing on the back of the map?"

Evan paused and lowered his gun slightly. "That foreign crap?"

Tillie continued, "I don't know where you grew up, but on the south side of Chicago, every kid was fluent in that language."

"Could care less," he replied, emotionless as possible.

"You should care. The words were in Pig Latin."

That caught Evan's attention, his expression twisted into a question mark.

Tillie continued, "The ink was smudged, but even I could figure it out. Prilay Ooolfay? It means April Fool in Pig Latin. Whoever created that treasure map did it as a prank."

Evan stood silent, his Beretta still pointed at the two women. Calculating his options, he decided to go with the fantasy of immediate wealth. Most people did. He said, "Get into the hole."

The noise behind him caused him to turn. Sasha was trying to figure out how to drive backwards with a manual transmission, but at too great a speed.

Evan yelled to her, "Hit the brakes!"

Tillie seized the moment. Like her heroine Wonder Woman did decades ago, she swirled the rope loop high in the air and let it fly. In her mind she saw it perfectly falling over Evan and she readied herself to yank it hard and drag him into the hole.

In reality, it simply fell at his feet. Evan glanced down at the pile of rope just as Sasha accidently hit the gas pedal instead of the brakes. The back of the van rammed into Evan, sending his body tumbling into the well. The vehicle's wheel did the same.

Tillie didn't know where Evan's gun landed, nor did she know if Sasha had one. She couldn't take the chance on finding out. "Run!" she yelled to Wyoming.

Tillie and Wyoming took off as fast as they could, while Sasha ground the gears again to get the van moving forward and the back wheel out of the hole. Sasha poked her head out the window and screamed, "Get back here and push."

Wyoming halted for a brief second before continuing her sprint, managing to make it to the road before Tillie. Wyoming ran down the road in one direction then stopped abruptly. Wyoming spun around and took off in the other direction. It took less than a minute for the police to capture her.

Behind Tillie, the van door opened. Sasha headed toward the woods while a police officer chased after her. It wouldn't be a problem for him to catch her. He wasn't wearing three-inch-high heels.

Betty leapt out of the squad car and raced toward Tillie. She asked, "Are you okay?"

"Yeah," Tillie responded, "Well, I'm sort of bummed ..."

Betty knelt down in the mud beside her friend and wrapped her arms around her. She said, "Who wouldn't be?"

213

Tillie's answer surprised her. "Yeah, it's tough to realize you're not Wonder Woman, after all."

"Yes, you are," Betty insisted, holding her tighter.

Tillie whined, "No, I'm not. If I were, my magic lasso would have worked, just like hers always did."

TWENTY-EIGHT

Betty took a bite of a sprinkle laden cake donut before saying, "They're men, Tillie. Codey and Buckley will never understand what a role model Wonder Woman is to us women."

"Champagne?" the server interrupted, carrying a tray of half-filled crystal glasses.

Pointing across the table Betty responded, "Sorry to say, not for either of us. We're on the clock." It was three hours before Tillie would sit behind the wheel of the Take A Chance tour bus while Betty boarded her passengers to head back to the Windy City.

Buckley responded, "I'll have a glass." For a change, Buckley wasn't dressed in his sheriff's uniform. It was the Sunday Champagne Brunch at Blackie's Buffet. Not only was he off of work, he was celebrating. Lifting his glass high in the air, he said, "To catching Deadwood's Most Wanted!"

Betty raised her water glass, Tillie her orange juice and Codey his coffee cup. Only the orange juice spilled on the table as the four vessels clanked in mid-air. Betty began to sop up the spilled liquid with her napkin when Hannah paused at their table.

Hannah asked, "Celebrating something?"

As far as Betty knew, except for the explosion at Harney's, Hannah had no idea of last night's activities. For now, it wasn't common knowledge that Tillie had been taken hostage on a wild goose chase, looking for seven hundred pounds of gold.

Betty answered, "In a way."

Hannah asked, "Did one of you win a jackpot?"

"Sort of," Tillie responded.

Betty was in such a jovial mood, she decided to go against her better judgment. "Care to join us, Hannah?"

Hannah shook her cotton ball like hairdo. "Jerome's waiting for me. "She pointed her cane toward a few tables over where Jerome stood, waving his hand for her to notice him.

"That's sweet," Betty responded. She'd never seen Hannah be as nice to anyone for so long.

"For now, but it won't be in a few minutes. I'm sending him packing," Hannah responded.

"Packing?" Tillie asked, wondering if Hannah already had the man handling her luggage for her.

Hannah stated, "I'm breaking up with him. I like keeping my options open. You never know what's around the corner, right Tillie?"

"Right," Tillie answered, tickled at the amorous adventures of her senior rider. "Got to know when to fold 'em."

"You're talking cards, right? Not legs?" Hannah asked and scattered away before Tillie could respond with a "Hannah!"

As soon as Hannah was out of earshot Betty added, "Their break-up should make for an interesting ride home."

"All of your rides are interesting, Mom," Codey said before adding, "Tillie, can we go back to what you were saying earlier? You lost me at Wonder Woman taught you to lasso?"

Tillie toyed with the jalapeno scrambled eggs on her plate. "She did. The magic lasso was her favorite weapon. Once it was tossed over a man, he couldn't do anything except tell the truth."

Betty quipped, "Too bad the magic rope doesn't really exist. If it did, it would change the world forever."

Tillie continued, "I was pretty good at lassoing in the third grade. Unfortunately, that was the last time I tried it, until last night."

Buckley winked, "I can see you as Wonder Woman."

Tillie responded, "Every year in school, I dressed like her for Halloween. I wore a gold headband decorated with a red star, a red and gold silky top, with a navy blue skirt with a million white stars. I carried the rope, and wore cardboard cuffs covered in gold foil wrapping paper that if they were like Wonder Woman's would deflect bullets." Tillie moved her two wrists back and forth to demonstrate the Wonder Woman technique.

"So that's where your fashion sense started," Betty teased.

"You may be right!" Tillie laughed. "Before I started watching the TV show, I preferred boring dungarees."

Buckley lifted his glass once again, "To Lynda Carter!"

"Hey, you know the actress' name!" Tillie said, surprised.

The sheriff responded, "It wasn't only girls who fantasized about her. Carter was my first celebrity crush."

Betty glanced at her watch. "This has been fun, but if I don't leave within the next fifteen minutes, I'll never finish what needs to be done so we can leave on time."

"Me too," Tillie stated, pouring her final stream of buttermilk syrup on her sunflower pancakes.

"Tillie, you're still going to drop by the station to make an official statement to my deputy?" Buckley inquired.

"You said it would only take a half hour?" Tillie asked.

The sheriff answered, "We've already tied up most of the loose ends in the investigation."

"No problem then," she answered.

Betty set her fork down. "Chad was arrested this morning and he's already been released on bail?"

Buckley explained, "The only thing we're charging him with is petty theft, but he's being punished. His grandfather's fired him from the hotel. His wife will likely be tossed in jail for decades."

Codey asked skeptically, "Are you sure you can make the theft charges on Chad stick? He didn't actually steal the items. Bella did."

Buckley responded, "That's where it gets tricky, legally speaking. But, he did train the dog to retrieve light weight items like purses or toys and bring them back home."

Betty shook her head in wonder. "And Chad thought having 'ghosts' steal items from hotel rooms would tempt tourists to stay at the hotel, rather than flee?"

Buckley answered, "It worked. Lame Johnny's is booked solid for the next year."

With a skeptical tone, Codey said, "If it worked so well, why did he abandon Bella outside of town?"

The sheriff answered, "It worked too well. The speculation the thief couldn't be a ghost was getting out of hand. Plus, Bella began breaking into homes via the doggie door. Chad was scared he'd eventually get caught."

"But there's no doggie door on a hotel room door," Tillie informed the table.

Buckley said, "No, but Bella would lie hidden on the bottom shelf of the linen cart Sasha pushed around. As soon as Sasha opened the door, Bella would bolt into the room, grab something and head back to the cart."

"Speaking of the woman…Murder One?" Betty asked.

Buckley answered, "Manslaughter. Her lawyer will probably claim it was an accident, or self-defense. But, we are charging both her and Evan with attempted kidnapping."

"Good," Betty stated, relieved to know that the two would pay for their crimes, one way or another. "And Wyoming?"

"Right now she's a cooperating witness, and will probably end up with probation only. We're convinced Sasha was hoping to shift the blame to her. That's why Sasha had her go to the hotel room, even though Johnson was already dead."

"That pretty much sums everything up into one neat package," Betty said, pleased with the sheriff's investigation, so far.

"Not everything," Codey added with a wicked twinkle in his eye. "Buckley, have you mentioned to Tillie what Chad told you about the air conditioning in the hotel?"

Buckley finished the last of his champagne and said, "Chad confessed he messed around with the air conditioning ducts. He claimed he was able to make the rooms colder in certain spots or release certain smells through the duct system."

"Floral scents," Codey added. "Probably lavender … meaning … there aren't any ghosts in this hotel. Only tampering by marketing gone bad."

Tillie folded her arms across her chest and stated bluntly, "Not buying it, not for even a second."

Codey said, "I thought you ghost hunters wanted absolute proof if a spirit existed, or it didn't."

Tillie answered, "This isn't proof of anything. I know what I smelled, felt, saw, and heard. Lame Johnny's and Harney's attic will always be haunted to me."

219

Codey teased, "Come on, Tillie. Even you have to..."

Tillie interrupted, "—The duct work doesn't explain the words 'Bella Come here' that we heard in Harney's attic.

"Perhaps Chad was walking Bella past the store at the time," Codey explained, "and he called out her name."

Tillie reiterated, "Nothing you can say will change my mind. Besides, what about the blood splattered gold nugget?"

The sheriff interrupted the friendly quibbling. "I can answer that. Actually that nugget is what started the bad feelings between Harney and his grandson. He was convinced Chad stole it from him, twenty some years ago. Chad has always denied it."

Tillie said, "See, proof again! The nugget was left there by ghosts."

Codey raised his hands in defeat. "I give up. There's no way I can convince you spirits aren't real."

"Just like I can't convince you the most important or improbable thing that you believe isn't real."

"And that is?"

"That the Chicago Cubs will never win the World Series."

Codey laughed, "You're right. You cannot convince me they will not win the World Series someday, in the future."

Tillie added, "In a galaxy far, far away."

∞

Both Betty and Tillie held their hands out to help Hannah onto the metal stairs leading into the tour bus.

"Did you have a good trip?" Betty asked.

"Good enough, won a few jackpots, someone gave me a nugget worth a hundred bucks."

"Jerome?" Betty asked, remembering the nugget he'd found panning for gold. He claimed he'd be buried with it.

"Maybe," Hannah answered. "But I like to keep my private life, private…"

And everyone else's public, Betty thought.

Before Hannah stepped onto the bus, she looked behind her and said, "I see we're going to have two new passengers."

"We are," Betty answered, smiling at the sight of her son walking with a chocolate Labrador and its puppy, both on leashes. "Their names are Bella."

"Both of them?" Hannah asked.

Betty nodded.

"Well, just make sure that neither one of them steals my purse," Hannah instructed and stepped inside.

Shocked, Betty asked Tillie, "How does Hannah know what happened? Did you tell her?"

Tillie answered, "I didn't say a thing but like you always say…"

The two women spoke at the same time, "Hannah knows everything."

"What does she know?" Codey asked, walking up to his mom. He was the final passenger to arrive for departure.

Betty reached down and petted the dogs simultaneously. She teased, "Hannah didn't tell us everything she knows, but I'm assuming she knows you and Christine are bringing juvenile delinquents into your home."

Codey smiled. "I'm planning on retraining them, but if that doesn't work, we'll make a heck of a lot of money at the reception."

221

Betty asked, "Did the sheriff find a home for the two German Shepherds?" Buckley promised to remove the animals from Chad's care as soon as possible.

Tillie answered instead, "He did. He's going to adopt them, himself. He insisted I visit the three of them when I come back for the trial, if not before."

Betty didn't mention that it appeared there was another man in Tillie's life. There always was.

Codey lifted the pup into his arm, and he and the dogs climbed on board. Tillie followed, waving at the busload of passengers who were already seated. She slipped behind the wheel and turned on the bus.

Betty looked around the city of Deadwood one more time. Even with all the excitement and terror, she loved the city. She vowed silently to come back. Next time she'd explore a few more places like Custer State Park or take a Black Hills aerial adventure. She might even try panning for gold. But before Betty returned, there were other tours already in the works. On the next tour, her niece Lori planned on traveling with her. And, if they could swing it, her office manager Gloria Morgan would tag along. The woman certainly deserved a vacation. And if they all traveled together, including Tillie, who knew what would happen?

But for now, the trip back to Chicago should be a good ride home. The rain had finally stopped, and the sun was shining. As Betty looked up at the Dakota skies one more time a glorious rainbow appeared.

A perfect ending, she decided, and stepped on board.

THE END

Buffet Betty's Blog

www.buffetbetty.com
Blackie's Buffet: Five Popped Buttons!

Wow! Wow! Wow! Our latest Take A Chance tour is barely over, and I'm already missing Deadwood, South Dakota. Life doesn't get any better than scrumptious local cuisine, gorgeous landscapes, winning slot machines, and finding "gold in them thar hills."

Our riders enjoyed reenactments of old time shoot outs on Main Street that were not only historically accurate, but provided laughs and chuckles. A few of our clients traipsed up to Mount Moriah to visit the gravesites of Wild Bill Hickok, Calamity Jane and other infamous figures from the Gold Rush era. Our driver, Tillie McFinn, stills swears Lame Johnny's hotel is haunted. As for me? I'm pretty sure it isn't.

But what about the number one reason folks go on a gambling junket? Yep—jackpots! We recorded a number of hand pays for our clients. For those who don't know what a hand pay is, it's when your jackpot registers twelve hundred dollars or more. A heck of a deal on a penny slot machine, for sure. Dozens of smaller jackpots were paid out, as well. In the bingo hall, three of our clients were able to yell out BINGO! They received cash prizes totaling over eighteen hundred dollars.

Do you want to know if I personally won a jackpot? I did—and it's one of my life's biggest! While on tour, my son Codey announced his girlfriend

Christine had accepted his marriage proposal. My son's engaged! We're having a wedding!

Codey asked me to be the official wedding planner for the dessert table at the reception. Already my mind is spinning with a million possibilities of goodies and delicacies. But for sure, I will include the incredible Sunflower Seed Oatmeal Cookie recipe that I've included for you. (Plus, the chef at Blackie's Buffet was kind enough to share a few more of my favorite finds, including directions on how to make chislic, South Dakota's original and legendary cuisine.)

Sadly, like on all tours, there were a few incidents we had to deal with that weren't so pleasant. But life is like that, isn't it? When you're dealt a bad hand, you learn to fold and hope the next one will be better. And know what? It usually is!

What do we have planned for our next tour? For the first time ever, Take A Chance tours is planning an eighteen hundred mile road trip! What could be worth such a long drive one way? The destination of course – Las Vegas, Baby!!!!! Not only am I thrilled to show my clients the casino and culinary delights of that city, but Tillie is totally psyched. She's convinced that aliens have landed in the desert outside of Sin City. And I'm pretty sure they haven't.

THE RECIPES

SUNFLOWER SEED OATMEAL COOKIES

Ingredients:
1 cup butter
1 cup brown sugar
1 cup granulated sugar
2 eggs
1 teaspoon vanilla
2 cups flour
1 teaspoon baking powder
¾ teaspoon salt
2 cups uncooked oats
2 cups unsalted, raw sunflower seeds
1 cup chopped walnuts

Directions:
Cream shortening, sugars, eggs and vanilla together. Add the remaining ingredients and mix. Roll into a long roll and wrap in waxed paper. Chill thoroughly in the refrigerator. When chilled, remove wax paper and slice into rounds. Bake at 350 degrees for around 10 minutes, or until the cookies are browned.

BUTTERMILK SYRUP

Ingredients:
1 cup of white sugar
½ cup of buttermilk
½ cup of butter
1 teaspoon baking soda
1 teaspoon vanilla extract

Directions:
Heat sugar, buttermilk, and butter in a saucepan over medium heat until mixture starts to boil, about 5 minutes. Remove saucepan from heat and stir baking soda and vanilla into buttermilk mixture. Note: this does foam up and bubble, so make sure you have a big enough pan to accommodate the heated contents.

LEMON AND SUNFLOWER SEED PANCAKES

Ingredients:
1 cup whole wheat flour
1 cup white flour
2 teaspoons baking powder
1 teaspoon baking soda
1 tablespoon sugar
½ teaspoon salt
½ cup unsalted, toasted sunflower seeds
2 large eggs
2 cups of buttermilk
2 tablespoons vegetable oil
2 teaspoons vanilla extract
2 tablespoons lemon zest, finely chopped

Directions:
Sift together the flours, baking powder, baking soda, sugar and salt. Stir in the sunflower seeds

In a medium bowl, whisk the eggs. Whisk in the buttermilk, canola oil and vanilla. Quickly stir in the flour mix and lemon zest. Do not overwork the batter.

Heat a griddle or a large skillet, either nonstick or seasoned cast iron, over medium-high heat. Brush with butter or oil. Use a 1/4-cup ladle or cup measure to drop 3 to 4 tablespoons of batter per pancake onto your heated pan or griddle. When bubbles break through the pancakes, flip them over and cook for another minute, until they are brown on the other side. Serve immediately.

COWBOY CHILI

Ingredients:

1 lb. boneless beef top sirloin steak, cubed into bite-size pieces

1/2 teaspoon salt

1/4 teaspoon ground black pepper

1 tablespoon Vegetable Oil

1/2 large onion, chopped

1 teaspoon finely chopped garlic

1 teaspoon Chili Powder

1 15 ounce can chili Beans

1 14 1/2 ounce can diced Tomatoes, undrained

1 10 ounce can diced Tomatoes & Green Chilies, undrained

1 6 ounce can tomato Paste

1 cup water

1 teaspoon granulated sugar

1/4 teaspoon ground red pepper

Optional toppings: Sliced green onions, sour cream, shredded Cheddar cheese, and crushed corn chips, optional.

Directions:

1. Sprinkle steak pieces evenly with salt and pepper.

2. Heat oil in 6-quart saucepan over medium-high heat 1 minute. Add steak pieces, onion, garlic, and chili powder. Cook 5 minutes, or until steak is browned on all sides and onion is tender, stirring frequently.

3. Add beans, both cans of diced tomatoes with their juice, tomato paste, water, sugar, and red pepper. Stir well. Bring to a boil. Reduce heat to low; simmer, uncovered, 10 minutes, stirring occasionally. Serve with optional toppings, if desired.

CHISLIC
(South Dakota Cubed Meat)

Ingredients:
1 lb. cubed lamb, venison or elk meat
2 teaspoons Worcestershire sauce
1 teaspoon chili powder
3/4 teaspoon salt
1/2 teaspoon garlic powder
1/2 teaspoon onion powder
1/4 teaspoon ground black pepper
oil for frying in pan

Needed:
Tooth picks

Directions:
Cube the meat. Put in a bowl add teaspoons.
Worcestershire sauce, chili powder, salt, garlic powder,
onion powder and pepper. Stir and marinate for one to
two hours. When marinating is complete, heat the oil
in a skillet or cast iron pan. Fry the cubes in batches so
they each get cooked through. The meat will be dark
brown and will be tender to the touch. Skewer the little
lamb cubes with toothpicks to serve. Serve with garlic
salt, hot sauce and traditional saltine crackers.

SHIRRED EGGS

Preheat oven to 375°

Ingredients:
1/4 teaspoon butter
2 teaspoons heavy whipping cream
2 eggs
Salt
Freshly ground black pepper
1 teaspoon minced chives
1 tablespoon Parmesan

Directions:
Coat a 6-oz. ramekin with butter.

Pour whipping cream into ramekin.

Crack eggs into ramekin, slowly pushing yolks toward the center, use a spoon if necessary.

Sprinkle eggs with salt and pepper, chives, and cheese.

Bake until set around edges and still a bit wiggly in the center, about 12 minutes. (Firmer yolks, bake an additional 3 minutes.)

Let sit 2 to 3 minutes to set and serve immediately.

.

ABOUT THE AUTHOR

Pat Dennis is the award-winning author of Hotdish To Die For, a collection of six mystery short stories where the weapon of choice is hotdish, deadly recipes included. Readers demanding more were rewarded with Hotdish Haiku, featuring 50 haiku and recipes from her and other writers. The Betty Chance mystery series includes: Murder by Chance; Killed by Chance and Dead by Chance.

Pat's short stories and humor appear in national magazine and anthologies, including Anne Frasier's Deadly Treats; Who Died in Here?; Silence of the Loons: Resort to Murder; Fifteen tales of Murder, Mayhem and Malice From the Land of Minnesota Nice; Once Upon a Crime Anthology; Writes of Spring; and Mood Change. The Witches of Dorkdom, a middle school fantasy and mystery novel was published under her pseudonym, Nora England. Pat performed as a stand-up comedian with over 1,000 performances at comedy clubs, Fortune 500 companies, Women's Expos, and special events. She has appeared on the same venue as Lewis Black and Phyllis Diller. Visit her at www.patdennis.com. For recipes, contests and restaurant reviews visit Pat and her alter ego "Betty Chance" and www.buffetbetty.com.

BOOKS BY PAT DENNIS

Murder by Chance
Killed by Chance
Dead by Chance
Hotdish To Die For
Fat Old Woman in Las Vegas: Gambling,
Dieting and Wicked Fun
Mood Change
Who Died in Here?
Hotdish Haiku

BOOKS WRITTEN AS NORA ENGLAND

The Witches of Dorkdom

ANTHOLOGIES / PAT DENNIS
Anne Frasier's Deadly Treats
The Silence of the Loons
Resort to Murder
Fifteen Tales of Murder, Mayhem and Malice
Once Upon A Crime Anthology
Writes of Spring
Cooked To Death

ACKNOWLEDGMENTS

A heartfelt thanks to my wonderful friends for their constant support and insight. Rhonda Gilliland, my top beta reader and friend. And my best buds who constantly put up with my continual whining: Marilyn Victor, Theresa Weir, Donna Seline and Peter Schneider. No one could ask for better friends. Nor could they ask for a finer, private, online writers' group that I lucky enough to be a member.